Acolyte to Priestess

The Twelve Crimes of Hannah Smith Series

Crimes 1 to 6

By Alp Mortal

Copyright © 2024 The Alderbourne Press Ltd

Written by Alp Mortal

Cover Design by Alp Mortal

Disclaimer: The material in this book is for mature audiences only and contains graphic content. It is intended only for those aged 18 and older. This is a work of fiction. All of the characters, places and events portrayed in this novel are either products of the author's imagination or are used fictitiously.

Published by

The Alderbourne Press Ltd

Falmouth, Cornwall, UK

2024

Author's Note

The Twelve Crimes of Hannah Smith is a series of crime stories, following the stellar fortunes of art thief Hannah Smith.

Acolyte to Priestess contains the first six of Hannah's twelve crimes, each charting the *on-the-rise* career of arch thief Hannah Smith.

... Hannah got back into the car and drove down the driveway towards the gates, which did not open immediately; she waited. Eventually, they did open, and she waved as she drove out; it had been touch and go all along. Her relief in not having to ram the gates and pay out for the damages to the car was palpable ...

Audacious, brilliant and cunning, Hannah may have fallen into thievery but having tasted of the forbidden fruit, no other path offers anything quite as sweet as the chance to alleviate the rich and powerful of their most treasured possessions.

The Twelve Crimes of Hannah Smith, of which *Acolyte to Priestess* charts the first six, and of which *Goddess to Infinity* charts the second six (scheduled to appear in 2025), are the prequel to the crime trilogy, *The Virtue of Dishonesty*, which will appear later in 2025.

Thank you,
Alp Mortal

Crime One - Possession is Nine-Tenths of the Law

Chapter One – Introducing Hannah

"Very good, Hannah ... lift your chin a little ... that's right ... and turn ... extend the arm a little more ... perfect!"

Madam clapped her hands and gave everyone five minutes to recover. Hannah's calves ached like hell but she didn't show it or complain. Dancing came naturally to her; she had rhythm and poise a plenty, a good ear for the music and bags of expression all of which was only equalled by her desire to be the best - which she was, as far as Madam was concerned and she'd seen plenty of young dancers in her time.

The rest of the group mingled, leaving Hannah to herself. She liked it that way. Hannah was never one to get too close to anyone; she wasn't haughty just reserved and maybe a little shy.

"From the beginning!" boomed Madam and they practised for another hour before being dismissed.

"Hannah ..." said Madam as Hannah was getting ready to leave, "... if you have a moment I would like to speak to you ..."

Hannah grabbed her things and followed Madam into her private rooms. The dance studio formed part of her private home, connected via a door from the hallway; the house was in Clapham, overlooking the Common.

"Yes, Madam ..." ventured Hannah, wondering what the old woman could possibly want with her.

"My dear, don't look so worried; I have a treat for you ..."

The old woman, French by birth and as graceful as a gazelle, handed her a thick piece of paper - an invitation.

"What is it?" asked Hannah, seeing words but making not head or tail of them yet.

"A private party; they would like you to dance, with a partner ... I think Gerald. Something classic yet with a twist. It's a hundred pounds for you and you will meet some very fine people."

"When?"

"Saturday ..."

"I'll need to get the night off."

"Let me know if you can't ..."

Hannah worked in a cocktail bar in the West End most nights to make ends meet; paying the rent on a tiny but chic little room just off the Edgware Road, paying Madam, attending deportment classes and language classes, shorthand, book-keeping and commerce and endless other things. No other seventeen-year-old girl did more to improve her prospects in this life than Hannah. She came from Ventnor on the Isle of Wight and had been in London for six months; ostensibly to learn to dance. However, the big city and the bright lights offered so much more to the girl who dreamed of being someone, a *somebody* - not in the public eye – but nevertheless, a mover and shaker behind the scenes. She'd have done very well as a Parisian salon hostess *and* she played the piano too.

Not a plain girl by any means but if you asked, "Oh; what does Hannah look like?" The person asked would struggle for a minute to pinpoint that feature that set her apart from the crowd. If she wanted to, she could melt away. Conversely, dressed and made up she could look like a million dollars *and* felt very comfortable in it. Naturally graceful and stylish, lithesome, a dancer, strong and agile, highly competitive and very, very intelligent; perhaps too intelligent for her own good and often, as a result, bored and restless, hence the myriad of courses and classes.

A day later she phoned Madam, "Madam, I can get the night off ..."

"Excellent! And Gerald can make it too ... practice on Friday from four to six."

"Thank you, Madam ..."

Chapter Two – Hawksbill

The name of the house and the family which resided there was 'Hawksbill'. The master was a big thing in banking; the mistress was the equivalent of that salon hostess and she moved and shaked behind the scenes to ensure the very finest people graced her soirees. The profit was considerable; the currency, information. She was the *hawk* in this relationship and Hannah admired her instantly.

"My dear child; come in out for the rain and let me fetch you a glass of champagne," she said as Hannah was admitted by the housekeeper but Madam kept her *hawk's* eye on the vestibule likewise the salon *and* the study where her husband was wheeling and dealing with some European investors. "Your partner has telephoned to say that he cannot make it and Madam Perrot cannot find a replacement at such short notice. Time for you to shine, my dear; don't worry, you'll do just fine. Madam suggests the competition piece which you have been working on."

"Oh, no, that's fine; I just need to loosen up ... but what about the music?"

"I can play for you; it's a piece I adore as it happens. Let me show you where you can change ..."

Francis escorted Hannah to a room upstairs where she could change and loosen up for fifteen minutes.

"Come down when you're ready, child, and relax!"

Easier said than done when you have fifteen minutes to polish a dance which you've only been working on in your spare time, with a pianist you don't know and a room full of people equally alien. Still, Hannah was always up for the challenge and she preferred to dance alone ... and if Gerald canned then she would get his hundred pounds too. These thoughts entertained her as she made her preparations.

She changed into her pretty costume and loosened up, performing a series of stretching exercises, then she checked her makeup and hair and judged herself to be ready. She descended and entered the main salon, catching the mistress's eye who then marshalled everyone to take a seat, leaving the floor to Hannah. Francis took up position at the piano and after a few bars to get her fingers loose she signalled to Hannah that she was ready and the performance began.

A simple country dance spiced with something exotic; a bit like your favourite meat and vegetables cooked in a deliciously aromatic sauce; you looked at it doubtfully until you'd taken the first bite then you couldn't get enough and before long the platter was clean and you were looking for second helpings. The performance lasted twenty minutes or so and the applause was warm and enthusiastic; pianist and dancer took a bow and for the last five seconds Francis stepped away and gave the floor back to Hannah to accept her due praise.

Thinking no one would actually wish to speak to her directly, she made to leave the room but two or three women waylaid her and very soon Hannah was mingling, veritably dancing through the crowd until she came across the master of the house, Gareth Hawksbill, the banker.

"My dear, that was delightful and wonderfully entertaining; won't you come into the study and I'll give you your fee ..."

She accepted his arm and was escorted to the study where two or three European banker types were ensconced with heavyweight tax papers; they didn't pay her any attention.

"Here you go, my dear child; and Francis insists you have something extra for your bravery in going solo at such short notice."

He handed her a thickish envelope.

"Thank you, Mr Hawksbill!"

"Call me Gareth; my colleagues missed a treat but as you can see, they are pouring over the latest tax regulations from Strasbourg. Thank God Maggie has them by the scruff of the neck else we shouldn't make a penny!"

Now Hannah was studying business finance so her question was well aimed and it grasped everyone's attention.

"If Sterling rises much more against the Dollar then wouldn't you do better to bundle into Yen futures?"

A colleague, possibly Spanish, looked at her directly and said, "The young lady might have a point." at which point Francis materialised.

"There you are, my dear; come and speak to the Foreign Secretary and leave these boys to their balance sheets and I think Hettie has a proposition for you ..."

And that was how the evening was; a waltz of a different kind. Having one's fingertips kissed by the Foreign Secretary was most definitely the highlight as far as Hannah was concerned ... but that was before she had opened the envelope!

Hettie was a favourite of the Hawksbill's; originally a Lancashire lass who had inherited millions from her grandfather; an art collector and seasoned socialite.

"Hannah; I have a gathering in two weeks' time, and I would be delighted if you would come and dance for us and of course feel free to bring a guest and enjoy the party afterwards ..."

"I would love to ..."

Hannah said goodbye and disappeared into the Notting Hill night, grabbing a bus rather than risk scuffing the heels of her favourite shoes though she toyed with the idea of a cab but promised herself she wouldn't open the envelope until she was safely behind her door. Her mother called her 'my little squirrel'.

If Hannah excelled at dancing then she certainly excelled at hoarding; just about anything of value that she came across - a Limoges tea cup, a pair of gloves by Chanel, antique lace, a first edition of 'Wuthering Heights', pieces of hand-painted silk, ivory figures, a jade lotus flower and so on. She had an eye for quality even when it was encrusted with grime and dust.

In her room she flung herself down on the bed and opened the envelope to find that it contained five hundred pounds.

"Sorry, Gerald; you missed out there!" she said to herself, and she placed the notes in a box, roughly the same size as a tissue box, which she kept under a loose floorboard by the radiator. There was already quite a stack in there before the five hundred was deposited.

"One day, Hannah," she mused, looking longingly at a print of a Degas painting of a ballerina which she'd found in Portobello Market that she'd hung on the wall by the window.

On Sunday, by way of a reward and celebration, she took herself to the Ritz to have tea and took in the last performance of *Forgotten Land* by Kylian at Sadler's Wells.

Well, it was her eighteenth birthday!

Chapter Three – Hettie

Two weeks later and she was knocking at the door of Hettie's smart house in Portman Square, accompanied by William, her closest and gayest friend. Hannah had no girlfriends and William was practically her only pal. He worked in theatre and regularly did her hair and makeup for performances and competitions. They were shown into the small *salon* where Hannah could change and William could put the final touches to her makeup.

"Jesus! Have you seen the stuff?" he exclaimed, eyeing every kind of antique *stuff* with which the house was literally bulging at seams.

"She's a collector and fabulously wealthy; have you seen the canapés waiter?"

"Yes, and he's fairly well bulging too but I don't stand a chance ..."

"Certainly not with an attitude like that; he's pretty but no prettier than you ... just smile ..."

"Yeah! Maybe I will ..."

Hannah was performing solo again and the crowd was larger. Hettie didn't play so had hired a pianist. It was someone Hannah knew, and she felt more confident, and the piece was one she had practised more often.

"Am I ready?" she asked William.

"Yup! I wish everyone was as easy to make up as you. Your face is just so ... so adaptable to so many styles. I bet you could even pass off as a man if you wanted to-"

"Thanks!"

"I didn't mean it like that; you're beautiful ..."

Hannah kissed him on the cheek.

"Go and grab some canapés!"

She made her way out and Hettie commandeered her for a second to re-introduce her to the pianist and of course to Francis and Gareth. They smiled and wished her well.

"Would everyone take their seats, please," announced Hettie and after a few minutes of bustle, the floor was Hannah's.

The piece was very contemporary and edgy; the moves were subtle and intricate, full of expression and based on a Greek tragedy, 'Electra' by Euripides. The dance was physically very demanding, and Hannah loved to push herself to the limit without making it look like it cost her any effort. Her body caught everyone's attention, not just the men's. However, one man in particular paid her more than his fair share. Rathbone was his name. The piece ended with a 'chaotic splurge' - Hannah's own words. The applause was hearty and lasted for three or four minutes, during which Hannah bowed and then invited the pianist to accept his due praise.

"My dear; that was wonderful!" exclaimed Hettie, "Come! Get yourself a glass of champagne and by all means stay for the party but let me pay you first ..."

She escorted Hannah to her study and retrieved an envelope from her desk which she handed over.

"You are very talented, Hannah; is dancing your chosen career?"

"Oh; I don't know; perhaps ... but there is so much I want to do and see. I love to dance but I want to travel and find excitement!"

Her eyes were shining, and her hands were immediately animated but then she became shy and blushed deeply.

"My dear; the World is your oyster. If you can dance like that then you'll never go hungry ... Do you like art?"

"I like some art. I especially like Degas because he painted such wonderful pictures of dancers ..."

"Come with me; I have something to show you."

Hettie looked practically conspiratorial as she towed Hannah to a first floor sitting room - seemingly her own private retreat – and on one of the walls was a painting of a ballerina. Hannah needed no clues to see that it was a Degas.

"It's beautiful!" exclaimed Hannah, automatically stepping up to it.

"It's an original; it was the first piece I acquired when I began to collect. It reminds me to follow my dreams ..."

"I have a print of a similar picture in my room. It reminds *me* to follow mine."

"Having and following dreams is easier when you're young; especially when you have talent. I have money but the dreams get lost in the 'noise'; everyone wants to talk ... and I shouldn't neglect my guests. I imagine more than a few will want to speak to you. Was that your boyfriend who you arrived with?"

"William; no, he's just a friend. I don't have a boyfriend ..."

"Make them dance, child!"

They quit the little room and re-joined the other guests in the main *salon*. Hannah sought out William.

"I've got our money; we don't have to stay. Did you catch his eye yet?"

"Yes, and he ignored me."

"Well, there's a guy standing by the fireplace who is eyeing you up; go and talk to him."

"What do I say?"

"Just say something like "did you enjoy the performance?" and take it from there."

"Oh, Christ, Hannah!"

"Do it!"

He left and for a moment Hannah was alone and just as she was about to look around for an inviting face, Rathbone was in front of her.

"You are a wonderful dancer, young lady; well done ..."

"Thank you," replied Hannah, smiling prettily.

"I'm Rathbone ..."

"Hannah ..."

"Are you a professional?" he asked, and he never took his eyes from hers.

"No; but I'm training ... Actually, I'm a cocktail waitress and studying; languages and business finance."

"So that?"

"I don't know exactly. I was going to talk to Gareth about it; he's in banking."

"Yes, he is and very successful; but once you're on the greasy pole you feel - I'm sure - that you have to stay on at all costs ..."

"And you?" asked Hannah, feeling strangely confident talking to this man who was at least three times older than her.

"I prefer to fly! Work freelance; never tied down."

"Doesn't that get a bit lonely?"

"Never; in any case, I prefer to sleep alone-"

"Me too!" admitted Hannah and then realised she'd divulged something very private about herself and blushed again.

"Don't blush, child; though you're prettier for it. Did she show you the *Degas*?"

"Yes; she did. It's beautiful," replied Hannah, recovering quickly.

"I want it, but she won't sell."

"She said it was the first piece that she'd acquired."

"Yes it was; she out bid me for it and it has plagued me ever since. That was twenty years or more ago, but I just can't get over it."

"She doesn't need the money ..."

"No, hardly; I wonder what *would* persuade her to sell ..."

Hannah said nothing, knowing next to little about Hettie and what might motivate her that way. She was intrigued by Rathbone, practically mesmerised by him and found it difficult to take her eyes from his despite the fact that it must have appeared to everyone else that she was thus enamoured.

"My dear, I'm hogging you; you should mingle and get yourself another gig out of this. We'll meet again," he said and then disappeared, leaving Hannah a little dizzy but fortunately William came back to rescue her.

"He wants me to go back with him; shall I go?" he asked.

"Of course! Help me to get changed and I'll give you your share then we're free to fly."

"And you?"

"I prefer to sleep alone ..." but she wasn't really answering him as she caught sight of Rathbone as he left the salon. He darted like a cat and then melted like a shadow. Only then did she realise that despite having spent five minutes looking into his eyes that she couldn't recall what colour they were.

Hannah mingled a little but picked up no fresh invitations; she didn't mind, her head was whirring with lots of other things. Rathbone dominated her thoughts and his quest, as yet unsuccessful, to liberate the *Degas* from Hettie that he so sorely wanted for his own.

Hettie was the last to speak to her before she decided to leave.

"I saw you talking to Rathbone, my dear. Be careful around him; he has a way of making you admit to things you'd rather you hadn't."

"Yes; he was a little disarming ... A great admirer of your Degas."

"Oh, what that man wouldn't give to have it; but I'll never sell it. Even when I die, I'll leave it to the Nation rather than see it hung over his mantelpiece ..."

Hannah left and was plagued by the 'uncharitableness' of what Hettie had said; why would she deny him the picture even in death? Back home she deposited her fee in the box - another five hundred pounds - and resisted the temptation to count the contents.

"Just wait, Hannah," she said to herself.

Instead, she meditated on her Degas. In the few minutes before sleep came to her the most amazing thing happened which hadn't happened since childhood. In her head, in her mind's eye, she saw a box drawn by an invisible hand and when the cube had been drawn it got labelled "Rathbone" and from the box extended a line to another box being drawn which got labelled "Hettie" and a line extended from her to a box called "Degas's picture". More lines and more boxes got drawn and suddenly there was an array of boxes and lines all interconnected and despite the bewildering collection she saw a sense in it and then, just a second before she dropped off, she saw it, the means to get the Degas for Rathbone.

Chapter Four – Honest as the day is long

Hannah came from solid stock; her father was a doctor, and her mother was a schoolteacher. She was an only child but despite that she'd never been spoiled - and in fact her parents were a little too strict if anything. They loved her and cared for her until she had said that she wanted to leave and pursue a career as a dancer. Then they supported her to find the room and the class with Madam but beyond that it was very much the case of "the rest is up to you". She loved them but knew she'd never inhabit their world and the island was very small; much too small for a bird with wings and a desire to use them.

She'd never done a dishonest thing or told a lie so the connection and the thoughts about how someone could get Rathbone the Degas were a great surprise to her, almost frightening, more so because she believed she wouldn't have had those thoughts had it not been for the encounter with Rathbone. He had unlocked something, liberated something; indeed, had freed her mind. What she couldn't really work out was why she felt *that* motivated to get it for him. He and Hettie were, in fact, playing a game and it was only a beautiful picture - Rathbone could have purchased others since and he had in fact.

She did feel Hettie was being uncharitable; just another level to the game she mused but the sticking point was what she would get out of it. If she did it then money was the obvious answer. She knew she needed money for the life she wanted to lead but to just do it for money seemed, well, ugly, base and plain criminal in fact. Only then did she feel the adrenalin flow as she pictured herself actually doing it; she felt the rush and her heart was racing and skipping beats.

"I must see him!" she said in desperation.

She had no means to find him easily of course and she didn't feel it was '*politique*' to apply to Hettie for the man's address, so she cogitated and sought out William to find out how his night of passion had gone.

"Oh my God!" were his first words.

"Are you going to see him again?"

"You bet; he's amazing!"

"Spare me the details; I just hoped you were okay."

"Did you get another gig?"

"Not exactly; there might be something in the pipeline though ... Shall we walk?"

They toured Covent Garden to see the street performers and enjoy the early summer sunshine.

"Do you know that man I was talking to; Rathbone?" she asked on the off chance.

"No; but the guy I was with said he was pretty shady. He has a shop in Angel; an antiques shop apparently. Hugh thinks it's just a front for handling stolen goods."

"Why does he think that?"

"He overheard that woman Francis say to Hettie that she should count the spoons - or something like that ..."

As they were walking and talking, the *thing* happened again and the "shop" got its own box and some lines got added and whereas before, everything new had a colour but the colours looked pretty randomly assigned, now the stronger links and most important information started to get colour-coded, making it easier to see.

The couple parted and Hannah headed immediately to Angel to find the shop; she thought she'd know it as soon as she saw it and she was right, a rather curious little place, tucked away and caught in a web of shadows. It was open. She looked in the window at the equally curious collection of antiques and suddenly Rathbone was at her shoulder.

"My dear! What a nice surprise; won't you come in?"

"Hello, Rathbone," she said, and she didn't recognise the voice which left her mouth: a much older voice and laden with secrets.

He smiled and showed her in.

"Tea?" he asked quaintly.

"Love some ..." she said absently as she gazed around the shop at the displays. Nothing was quite what it seemed; closer inspection told you, for example, that the cute little portrait of a Victorian child was painted on an actual piece of mummified human skin - apparently the child's own, having died from Typhoid fever. It left Hannah feeling 'unclean' but altogether fascinated.

"What do you see that you really, really want?" Rathbone asked as he handed over the cup and saucer.

"The powder compact there," Hannah said, pointing at the article in a little display case which held other similar things.

"Ah! Yes, well spotted ... accredited to Fabergé ... a pretty little thing. You have an eye and taste; so unlike most young women I know. They always want something big and chunky, and the gaudier the better ..."

"How much is it?" asked Hannah.

"Ten thousand pounds," he replied as he fished it out and handed it over to her.

"Is it gold?"

"Yes, and his monogram is enamel; it's genuine ..."

She held it up and opened the lid and checked her face in the little mirror like she was the Tsarina herself. She handed it back and just smiled but then added, "Why do want the *Degas* so badly?"

He seemed caught off guard momentarily and refocused to gain his composure again.

"It speaks to me; as plainly as you - it has a soul. I barely think about anything else," he admitted, and he was surprised by how so easily he'd let slip something so personal to this complete stranger.

"What would you give to have it?" Hannah asked, looking directly into his eyes which she saw were green with dark halos around the pupils; a fact she *registered* and would now never forget.

"Practically anything; this shop and everything in it ... my soul ..."

"If I said I could get it for you, what would you say?"

"I wouldn't say *how* but I would ask *why*."

"Because you desire it for the right reason."

"And Hettie doesn't?"

"She's a collector; it's vanity – 'I have a 'Degas' - it's a soulless motive for wanting to keep it."

"But it's hers ... and to steal it would be wrong," Rathbone added, feeling slightly out of his depth, "and in any case, if someone did then all fingers would point at me ..."

"For twenty-five thousand pounds and the Fabergé compact, I could guarantee that you would have good title to it."

"And you?"

"I'll have what I really, really want and no one will suspect me."

"You play a dangerous game, young lady ..."

Hannah smiled and added, "I need a prop; something small and apparently valuable ... the lipstick case ..."

"A fake but nonetheless looks the part."

"Let me have it and in a week, on Sunday afternoon, at three o'clock, meet me at the entrance to the Physic Garden and have the money and the compact with you. I'll hand you the painting and a receipt that shows that you bought it from Hettie; one she won't be able to deny issuing ..."

"And if you fail?"

"I won't but if I do you will have lost nothing more than a worthless bauble ... What is your surname?"

"Lawe."

"Are we agreed?"

He hesitated but masked it by ferreting in the display cabinet for the lipstick case.

"For some strange reason, I trust you and believe in you; a rare commodity both. We are agreed; twenty-five thousand pounds and the compact for the picture and a receipt signed by Hettie herself ..."

"Then I will see you next Sunday; please don't be late."

"Have no fear of that …"

Hannah plucked the lipstick case from his fingers and popped it in her bag.

"Thank you!" she said, and she left, hot footing it immediately to Hettie's in Portman Square. What amazed her more than anything was her energy. She seemed to be running on pure adrenalin; it kept everything sharply focussed yet despite that, her breathing was quite normal.

She arrived at Hettie's and the housekeeper answered the door.

"Is Hettie at home? It's Hannah."

"I'm sorry, my dear, she's out. What was it you wanted?" asked the woman, a mature old bird who looked like *Miss Marple* - a thought which gave Hannah a smile on her inward-looking face.

"I think I dropped my lipstick case here last night when I got changed; I was hoping someone had found it …"

"Come in, my dear, and we'll look for it. I haven't seen it, but Gordon might and Mrs Braithwaite is due back at five; have a cup of tea won't you?"

"Thank you; if it isn't too much trouble."

"None at all," she said, trailing off as she waddled in, leaving Hannah to close the door behind herself.

Chapter Five – All that glitters is not gold

Shakespeare actually said "glisters" but let's not split hairs. Hannah was escorted to the kitchen where the housekeeper – Margaret - introduced her to her husband, Gordon. They kept house for Hettie and apparently, they had a family connection; a stalwart Lancashire couple with few airs and graces but loyalty in buckets.

"Gordon; the young lady lost a lipstick case last night; did you come across it by chance?" she asked her husband.

"Where might you have dropped it, young lady?" he asked.

"I changed in the small *salon,* but Hettie showed me the *Degas* upstairs ... perhaps in either of those two rooms."

"The small salon has been vacuumed today but the small room upstairs is Mrs Braithwaite's private sitting room and cleaned less often; most likely it is there. I'll go and have a look whilst Margaret gets you a cup of tea ... Mrs Braithwaite was very taken with your performance last evening."

"Thank you," said Hannah politely as the man shuffled off in the direction of Hettie's private boudoir.

"There you go, my dear; a nice cup of tea. So, tell me a little about yourself; are you from London?"

For the next ten minutes, Hannah told Margaret her short life history up to the point of the performance the evening before.

"And what of your plans, my dear?"

"Become a really good dancer and maybe travel ..." said Hannah and it was largely still how she felt most of the time, but the world seemed only ever to grow and her dreams expand with it, "I'd also like to study art; like the fine painting in the room where I dropped my lipstick."

"Speaking of which, where is Gordon?"

"Perhaps I should go and help him; it might have rolled under the sofa."

"Would you, my dear? I have to start dinner."

Hannah left the old woman and went up to the first-floor room where Gordon was hunting for the lipstick.

"Margaret said I might help you, Gordon; it could have rolled under the sofa ..."

"To be honest, child, I can't see so well, especially in this dim light she has the room in - to protect the painting apparently. If you want to look, I'd be grateful; these knees of mine aren't what they were."

"That's fine ..."

Margaret called up for Gordon whose assistance she needed.

"I'll be fine ... if it's not under the sofa then it isn't here and I'll call it lost," she said, subtly adapting her pattern of speech to match his; it garnered his confidence.

"Right you are ..."

He left to render his good lady wife some assistance and finally Hannah was alone in the private boudoir of Hettie Braithwaite. She sat at the desk and tried the drawers which opened to her amazement. Carefully lifting everything out, she found Hettie's most personal of things, including her diary and the inventory of the collection which she had amassed over the last twenty years. Hannah pulled it out and opened it at the first page to see the entry for the Degas which Hettie had said had been her first purchase ... and sure enough it was the first entry.

Hannah quickly scanned the pages for acquisitions and disposals and, confirming her suspicion, found the entry for the disposal of the Degas some ten years later; a private sale to an overseas collector.

"It is a fake!" she said to herself. She heard Gordon's feet on the stairs and quickly put everything back, throwing herself on the floor, wedging her arm under the sofa.

"Have you found it?" he asked as he entered the room.

"It's here!" she gasped and at that precise moment withdrew her arm and held up the lipstick case for him to see.

"Well done! Mother has taken a cake out of the oven; come and get a piece whilst it's hot."

Hannah descended behind him, and the full plan now filled her head and it put a beautiful smile on her face.

"You found it, my dear; what a pretty thing. I'm not surprised you wanted to find it," said Margaret as she dispensed more tea and a piece of warm plum cake.

Hannah left before Hettie showed up and made her way to the house of her dance teacher to hatch the plan.

"If we put on the performance then I'm sure Mrs Braithwaite will lend us the painting for the evening ..."

"It's an idea ... and to stage the performance for charity will certainly tug at the heart strings. Let me call her and ask her."

Hannah's idea was to stage a dance performance for charity, and it was her proposal to dress as the ballerina in the *Degas* and bring it to life. Now that Hannah knew for certain that the *Degas* was fake, she was pretty sure that Hettie would not want the picture to be viewed because there was always the risk that the overseas collector would find out and then her charade would be exposed. Hannah planned to pose as a collector and offer to purchase the *Degas* from her so that Hettie could be rid of the potential embarrassment and have the perfect excuse not to show the painting.

Hannah mused that Rathbone didn't know that the picture was a fake and he'd be buying a copy for twenty-five thousand pounds *plus* the Fabergé compact. When he found out; if he ever did, then of course he couldn't say anything because his reputation would be in tatters too.

Chapter Six – The stage is set

Mrs Braithwaite would be delighted to exhibit the painting for the evening as centre piece for the performance which Hannah would dance, so said Madam a few days later; and now Hannah needed to act very quickly. She planned to get William to do her hair and makeup, oriental style. She borrowed a very chic outfit from a dance colleague and practised her accent; English spoken by a young Japanese businesswoman. It was the hardest thing she'd ever done and frequently lapsed but she practised for hours. She telephoned Hettie a few days later to set up the appointment for the possible purchase, and sure enough Hettie would only be too pleased to meet with her. When Hettie asked how she knew that she had the *Degas*, Hannah replied that a business associate of Gareth's had mentioned it.

The appointment was set for two days hence, on the Friday, at eleven in the morning at the house in Portman Square. Hannah got a business card mocked up with her name *'R Lawe - Consultant International Tax Adviser'* printed on it with a fake telephone number and an address in Hong Kong.

Hannah studied herself in the mirror for hours and once William had done her makeup and put her hair under a wig which was called, apparently, a 'power bob', she didn't recognise herself.

The riskiest part of the plan was getting Hettie to write out a receipt for the picture, without having got any money for the painting. But Hannah was going to suggest that if Hettie could wait until the Monday, then the exchange rate of yen to sterling would be in her favour but a receipt was necessary in order to arrange insurance. She knew Hettie wanted shot of the picture so there was motivation on her side to conclude the deal and get the offending article out of her possession before she was required to hand it over for the gala.

Hannah made her way to Portman Square for the appointment and took a cab just in case Hettie was looking out for her; it looked more professional she thought. The first hurdle was whether Margaret would recognise her; she was sure Gordon wouldn't. If she could fool Margaret, then she felt much more confident.

She rang the bell and took a very deep breath, said a Japanese proverb in her head three times and shot the cuffs of her crisp white shirt from the sleeves of her Chanel jacket.

Chapter Seven – All the World's a stage

Margaret answered and asked Hannah to come in, ushering her into the small salon, asking very politely if she would like tea. Hannah replied that if there was any jasmine tea, she would very gratefully take a cup else water. Five minutes later, Hettie came in and the test of the disguise - which had passed Margaret's inspection - was now under the full glare of the house lights.

So far so good as introductions were made and Hannah dropped the appropriate names into her opener to ensure that credentials were established pretty quickly. Then the invitation was extended to Hannah to view the picture and they adjourned to the small boudoir. Hannah knew Hettie wouldn't move it because the light was dim and that would mask the forgery should a very close inspection be requested.

"Payment on Monday would be fine, Ms Lawe, if, as you say, the exchange rate will work in my favour, and I have no reason to doubt it, and I can see the need for the receipt to organise the insurance but there is the question of the performance tomorrow night at which the picture was to be exhibited. Do you still plan to loan the piece to the dance company?" were Hettie's words as Hannah examined the picture and Hannah knew that Hettie didn't want the piece to be exhibited for risk of disclosure.

"No, Mrs Braithwaite; we do not plan to exhibit the piece. Perhaps the dance company could use another; maybe the *Toulouse Lautrec*?" was Hannah's question by return.

"If you purchase the piece then I will phone them straightaway and alert them to the change in the plan."

"I certainly do wish to purchase the piece," stated Hannah very confidently.

Hettie asked Gordon to wrap the picture and whilst he did so, Hettie took tea, jasmine, with Hannah in the small salon and it was the riskiest part of the plan as the room was bright. However, Hannah had worn a little pill box hat with a veil that just covered her eyes, and well-timed lapses into Japanese were designed to put Hettie in no two minds that *Ms R Lawe* was the genuine article, unlike the *Degas* that was delivered to them fifteen minutes later.

Profuse thanks were shared, and Hannah left, hailing a cab instantly.

In the evening, she spoke to Madam who explained to her that the *Degas* was no longer available, but they could have a *Toulouse Lautrec* instead and would Hannah mind doing a "can-can" inspired routine?

"Of course not, Madam; it's for charity and no one will complain."

And of course, no one did and hardly anyone paid the picture any attention at all whilst Hannah was high kicking and displaying her ample charms.

On the Friday and Saturday evenings, the *Degas* hung in her room where her print usually did; that was packed along with everything else she intended to take because after the handover she was off to Paris to study with a dance instructor recommended by Madam.

Chapter Eight – Adieu

Hannah was already at the entrance to the Physic Garden before Rathbone arrived; the picture was secured in a smart portfolio by her side, the receipt was in an envelope in her hand.

"Hannah," he beamed as he arrived, looking flushed with the anticipation.

She handed him the envelope which he opened, and he removed the receipt which he scanned rapidly.

"How did you do it?" he asked.

"It was just a matter of applying to Mrs Braithwaite's charitable side," Hannah replied, "but of course I played no part in this ..."

"No, no; of course not. Who would believe it anyway?"

"The picture is here," and she gestured to the portfolio, but she was really asking for her payment.

"May I see it?" he almost begged.

She handed him the case and he unzipped it just enough to see the picture within.

"I can't wait to see her," he said.

"Perhaps leave it a day or two, Rathbone; I believe Hettie is in mourning!" and Hannah winked.

"Yes; a little decorum I agree will go a long way ... here's your money and the compact."

He handed her a large jiffy bag which contained the thick wads of fifty-pound notes, and the compact wrapped in tissue paper.

"Thank you ..."

"You're not going to count it?" he asked.

"Should I?"

"No; it's all there."

"I have to go, Rathbone; I have a class," Hannah lied.

"Of course; and if you ever need anything in the future, please don't hesitate to call on me."

"I will; goodbye."

"Goodbye, Hannah."

She left and hailed a cab, asking the cabbie to drop her at Waterloo East.

She caught a train to Dover, thence took the ferry to Calais and the following day a train to Paris where she weaved her way to Montmartre and took up a room above a bakery on Rue Lepic, overlooking *Le Moulin de la Galette.*

Throughout the journey, she wondered just what Rathbone was going to say to Hettie and how Hettie would react. If Hettie went looking for the business card to prove to herself, if no one else, that she had been duped then she wouldn't find it; Hannah had lifted that off of the desk whilst Hettie had admonished Gordon for bumping the doorframe with the picture as he returned with it wrapped. So, Hettie couldn't deny it without a lot of questions and neither could she admit to Rathbone that it was a fake for her reputation would be in tatters and neither could he if he ever found out; a man of his calibre buying a fake; no one would take him seriously again.

As far as Hannah was concerned, Hettie got off lightly because she hadn't been swindled out of anything in reality and to get shot of the picture did her no end of favours for the most part; she could always deny selling the picture to Rathbone because she had a record of a genuine sale ten years earlier and assert that someone else had sold Rathbone the picture, forging the receipt.

Margaret and Gordon had seen the Japanese businesswoman leave with the picture but Hettie could always rely on their loyalty and who was to say which *Degas* the young woman had left with?

She did feel a little sorry for Rathbone; he had purchased a fake, but he thought it was real and it was what he really wanted; wasn't that enough? If he gloated to Hettie, then she too would know he had a fake and that might give her a private moment of satisfaction; or maybe she'd finally extend her charity to him and marry the poor bastard because it was what they both really wanted. Their denial was their weakness, masquerading as their power over each other. The games adults play mused Hannah.

Hannah was more than happy because the *Cartier* lipstick case she had pinched from Hettie's boudoir, seen on the evening of the performance, leaving the fake in its place, was worth at least five thousand pounds and together with the Fabergé compact and the bag stuffed with fifty-pound notes, she had somewhere in the region of five hundred thousand French francs and that made her very happy indeed.

Crime Two - Masquerade

Chapter One – Making friends and influencing people

Hannah had been in Paris for nearly five months and for the most part she had studied like she had in London, also finding some work in a theatre cloakroom some evenings. She worked less due mainly to the fact that she had the money Rathbone had paid her, although she was very careful with it. She needed the time to study more and the job at the theatre covered her basic expenses. Occasional dance performances allowed her to treat herself and the tips kept her in cigarettes, a habit which she knew she would one day regret forming but for the meantime she enjoyed it and especially so after she had found the perfect Cartier cigarette holder and case.

She scoured the flea markets, and there's nothing like Paris flea markets; ferreting out more Limoges cups and saucers until she had six then trading up. She was constantly increasing her capital and with shrewd investments, she earned a sizeable income for someone of her age with no real job. She still danced, still the greater of her two passions. The second was now Art, following her success in London. Gone was the sentimentality of the print of the pretty picture hanging above the bed; now it was hard-nosed research, and all came within her sphere. Values and appreciation rates, auction results and detailed profiles on collectors were her *pain beurre* most days.

Had it not been for the sheer unadulterated pleasure of stealing the *Degas* from Hettie - which still made her heartbeat faster - she probably would have called it a day. But she was hooked on the rush and a quarter of an eye was always open and seeking the next opportunity. Rathbone had been willing to pay almost anything to have the *Degas* and this time she wanted to play for bigger stakes and earn herself a bigger reward.

One thing bugged her. She had a passport in the name of *Hannah Smith* and if she wanted to pass herself off as someone else then an alternative identity was going to be necessary but that was something she didn't know how to get; until she met Boehme.

She was working the cloakroom one evening and a man came in and dumped his overcoat on the counter. Hannah handed him a numbered token and he handed over ten francs and then walked smartly into the auditorium, barely making eye contact. She picked up the overcoat to hang it on the appropriate hanger, but she inadvertently grabbed the bottom edge of the coat rather than the collar and as she pulled it off the counter, the contents of the inside pocket tumbled out; two passports and a business card - *Boehme Silvestre, Notaire*.

She picked up the card and passports and automatically looked in both for it seemed strange that he should have two passports and stranger still that he should have two passports both with the same picture in them but bearing different names. The picture was not of him, so these were not his. Did that mean he could get such things made? She put the passports and the business card back in the pocket.

After the performance, the gentleman returned to the counter for his coat and handed Hannah the token. She fetched the coat and handed it to him but held on to it for a second by way of grabbing his attention. He looked at her and she said in perfectly accented French, "Monsieur Silvestre; I am in need of your services ..."

He smiled, fished in his pocket for the card and handed it to her saying, "I am at your service, Mademoiselle."

She knew that he knew exactly what she wanted, and it wasn't assistance with a will or a house purchase. Only by finding the business card would she have known his name and if she'd found the card then she must have found the passports.

He handed her fifty francs and departed.

She'd felt the same rush; had experienced the same buzz; her heartbeat faster and she knew if she looked in the mirror, she would see her eyes gleaming and an apocryphal smile playing around the corners of her mouth.

The following morning, she telephoned his office and made an appointment for the following day. When the receptionist had asked for her name she said, 'Isabel Tissier'.

Chapter Two – Boehme Silvestre

The appointment with Boehme was at three o'clock, after lunch; so, in the morning, Hannah danced and went to the bedsit of a student with whom she exchanged English lessons for French conversation. He played the flute, and she sang for him occasionally if he needed a singer for a gig. Through these engagements, she got invited to spend the evening with some of the wealthiest Parisian families.

After lunch, she made her way to the offices of Boehme Silvestre which were on *Rue des Archives* in *Le Marais* above a letting's agent. She ascended the stairs and announced herself to the receptionist who asked her to take a seat.

Five minutes later, Boehme appeared in the reception area and asked her to step into his office. Hannah was more nervous than excited; nervous because she might have got it wrong but in any case, she was now in his office and momentarily stuck for the right words.

"You are in need of my services, Mademoiselle; is that right?" he asked, not looking at her until he had finished speaking and then he peered directly into her face.

"That is correct, Monsieur."

"I merely act as the go-between in these cases; all I need from you are the correct photographs and the details which will appear in the documents. A full set of official documents will cost ten thousand francs; two sets, eighteen thousand francs. I charge two thousand francs for my services ... is there anything you want to know?"

This was all spoken very plainly, and it reassured her.

"There is nothing I think I need to know. I will obtain the photographs and the details, and then hand them to you?"

"Yes; with full payment; delivery in ten days. When you come back with the information and the money, we will arrange the handover ..."

"Thank you, Monsieur."

"I ask no questions; it's easier that way. I must say that no one quite so young or beautiful has asked for my services before. Perhaps I should caution you that the penalty for, how shall we say it, 'being unmasked', is very severe ..."

"Thank you, Monsieur; I will be very careful."

"Right; come back with the things I need and the fee ..."

Hannah got up and went to leave.

"... I am attending the Opera tonight and I would rather not go alone; would you do me the honour of being my guest?" he added very earnestly.

Hannah blushed, having never been invited out in such a manner before, and she was dying to go to the Opera, but it was hellishly expensive.

"I would be delighted to accept your invitation and accompany you this evening."

"Excellent! Where shall I pick you up?"

"By the fountain in *Place des Innocents*."

"But of course! At 7pm," confirmed Boehme, chuckling to himself.

"7pm, Monsieur."

And with that, Hannah left.

She had just over three hours and raced to the theatre so her pal could do her hair and makeup *and* she needed a dress. She raced back to the room to get her smart clutch bag into which she placed her compact, lipstick case, cigarette holder and a full case of cigarettes, some money - around two hundred francs - and an embroidered handkerchief. She changed into the dress and donned an antique lace shawl since the evening promised to be warm.

In a little bar just off the square, she downed a brandy and then skipped to the fountain to find Boehme waiting, who duly presented her with a corsage and kissed the fingertips of her right hand.

"You look beautiful!" he announced gallantly, and Hannah just blushed again, giving him her arm.

They took a cab and en route he told her a little about the Opera, having guessed it was her first time. Then he asked her, "What do you do in Paris, Mademoiselle?"

"I am studying and taking dance lessons from Federico."

"He is highly respected; you must be very good."

"I have much to learn," replied Hannah in a voice as antique as the lace of her shawl.

They arrived and he escorted her into the building for the performance of 'La Boheme', and Hannah knew already she was going to enjoy the evening immensely. She was dressed at least as well as the other woman of her age and her partner was at least but probably more handsome than theirs. They made a very stylish couple; he a little older and well versed in etiquette; she like a rose in full bloom, thick velvety petals of antique cream tinged with strawberry freshness, fragrant but not too sweet.

At the interval, they had champagne and smoked a cigarette. She accepted one from his case and he lit it for her with his heavy, solid gold *Rollagas* which was monogramed 'BS'.

"Are you enjoying the performance?" he asked.

"Immensely; are you?" she replied.

"I don't remember the last time I enjoyed being here with someone so much ..."

"I am studying Art, but I have to confess that I have neglected Opera; I am more drawn to the costumes than to the singing."

"If costumes are your thing, then perhaps you would accept another invitation from me and accompany me to the masked ball at *Fayette's* this Saturday?"

"I would need to get another night off."

"Perhaps your days as a cloakroom attendant are coming to an end," he suggested cryptically.

"Perhaps they are. I would love to go to the ball ... but I will arrive alone, and you shall have to search me out."

"I shall have the invitation for you tomorrow when you come to the office ... Shall we go back in?"

They watched the rest of the performance, and he got her a cab to take her home, handing the driver a hundred francs for the fare.

"Until tomorrow; goodnight, Mademoiselle."

"Until tomorrow, Monsieur ..."

The cab drove away, and Hannah smiled to herself throughout the entire journey. The corsage he had given her was silk and she placed it on her dressing table.

The following morning, she went to the railway station and obtained the photographs that she needed. In both cases, she adopted a very plain look, nothing very attention grabbing. She had already written down the details that were needed and put the photographs in the envelope with the neatly written sheet of paper, together with twenty thousand francs in large bills. She made her way to the office and timed her arrival to coincide with the receptionist's departure for lunch. She ascended the stairs.

Boehme was in his office on the telephone, smoking a cigarette and drinking a glass of wine when she arrived in the reception. Initially he must have thought that it was his receptionist returning for he didn't curtail the call and he continued with the conversation. Hannah only heard half of it of course but it made for intriguing listening and from what she could tell, he was negotiating the fee for something to be acquired; the *thing* had not been mentioned specifically and was simply referred to as 'the piece'.

At one point he asked the question 'when?' but Hannah knew he had simply repeated the question of the other person because he went onto to say immediately, "Saturday, at the ball; no one will suspect." The call was ended and there was silence for a few minutes before he appeared in the doorway.

"Mademoiselle; you are here!" stated with an ounce of consternation.

"The receptionist was not here so I didn't know whether I should wait or knock," said Hannah, perfectly innocently.

"No; quite ...come through ..."

She went in and handed him the envelope which he took and placed in the drawer of his desk.

"Did you get the night off for the ball on Saturday?" he asked.

"I quit the job; it was beginning to interfere with my various occupations and projects," she said, smiling but drawing attention away from her face by offering him a cigarette from her case. He took one and then lit hers.

"You intrigue me, Mademoiselle, greatly; I wonder if I can trust you."

"Trust usually has to be earned, Monsieur."

"Quite so; how would I earn your trust?"

"By completing our business promptly and by telling me what it is you have been asked to acquire for one million francs ..."

"Our business will be completed satisfactorily, have no fear of that ... as to the other, if I tell you then I assume you have experience?"

"Yes, some; and I am keen to build on it ..."

"What do you know of the 'Fayette Chalice'?"

"At one time believed to be the *Holy Grail* itself but, in any event, a fine gold chalice, adorned with gems and brought back from the Crusades; gifted to the Fayette's by Richard for their part in his repatriation ..."

Hannah had already researched the Fayette's as soon as she had the invitation to the ball.

"That is correct, and you will see it on Saturday; at least, the copy which everyone believes is on display. No one in their right mind would display the original in a private residence; even one as secure as theirs ... I have been asked to acquire it for a client. They accept the risk that the chalice could be a copy but if it is then the family is barred from admitting that, seeing as a hundred thousand people a year pay twenty francs to see it ..."

Hannah garnered every fibre of her confidence.

"I can do it."

"There is no doubt in my mind that you believe that you can; whether you can pull it off is another matter. Success will earn you eight hundred thousand francs."

"And failure?"

"If caught then a very long jail sentence and you'd probably never get a job again, even in a theatre cloakroom."

"Then the risk is all mine."

"There could never be any trail back to me."

"How should I get paid?"

"The handover is almost immediate; you would be handed an untraceable bearer bond for the eight hundred thousand francs."

"Is your fee always twenty percent?"

"Invariably, and I am going to give you the twenty thousand francs back that you gave me earlier because you'll need it for the costume on Saturday; these things are legendary."

"I agree to do it for eight hundred thousand francs as long as the documents I need are with the bond at the handover ..."

"That is pushing it, but I agree ... I am taking a huge risk."

"So am I ..."

He opened the desk drawer and withdrew the twenty thousand francs from the envelope she had given him and handed them back plus the invitation she needed for the ball.

"The handover is at one in the morning on the platform of the *Argentine* Metro station, direction Chateau de Vincennes. The man to whom the chalice should be given will announce himself as 'Le Coeur de Lion' ..."

"How will he recognise me?"

"Not too difficult if you are still in costume, I should say."

"I hardly think that is wise; it would draw far too much attention. No, the handover will take place the following day at ten o'clock in the morning, here in this office, and I will hand it over to you; I trust no one else."

He paused and looked hard for a second or two and then said, "Agreed; if you had agreed to my suggestion then I would have judged you to be the novice that I thought you were; I am happy that isn't the case. Let's not forget that we have the ball to look forward to as well ... Are you still going to tease me and arrive alone?"

"Most definitely; but you won't be alone for long."

They heard the receptionist return and took that as their cue to conclude their business and Hannah left, heading straight for the Fayette residence where for twenty francs she was admitted to a public area of the house to view the chalice, along with fifty other tourists.

Then she went home.

Chapter Three – Preparing for Fayette's Ball

The ball was a Venetian Ball so the costumes were expected to be magnificent, and of course everyone would be wearing a mask ... but dressed in her costume was not how Hannah planned to arrive. She contacted the firm which was providing the catering staff and asked if they needed waitresses. Fortunately, they did and her passable Japanese and Russian, near native French and perfect English got her a job for the night ... having been a cocktail waitress for six months also helped. Being employed as one of the bar staff gained her entry to the house earlier than the guests and gave her access to areas which they were excluded from; and in Hannah's experience, a young cocktail waitress, running an errand for the bar manager, could get away with almost anything in the chaos which typified the 'behind the scenes' of these shindigs.

Her visit to the house to see the chalice had been to confirm that the piece was heavily protected; and it was. It was secured in a cabinet made of inch thick glass, cordoned off by a metal railing. A smash and grab raid this most definitely was not; at least, not in the usual style of such things. The room where the chalice was exhibited to the public was also under camera surveillance and two heavy-set security guards manned the entrance until six p.m when the public room was closed.

Her conversation with Boehme had taken place on the Wednesday lunchtime so she had two clear days before the ball and was only required to call into the office of the catering firm to sign a form and be issued with an ID badge. She organised her costume and went for 'the court jester'; deliberately androgynous and far less bulky to pack into a modest-sized holdall, and a darn sight cheaper to hire too! The single prop she needed was far easier to come by than she had anticipated; replicas of the chalice were on sale in the foyer of the public viewing room; sold by the cartload to the Japanese tourists. A fact which Hannah thought was incredibly tacky but at two hundred euros, a nice little side-earner for the Fayette's

On the Friday afternoon at three o'clock, she returned to the public viewing room and trudged around the display with another fifty tourists; this time dressed as a tourist.

She left the group to use the toilet. In the ladies' toilet there was a wastepaper basket for the paper towels that were provided to dry one's hands. She set light to the contents and quickly made her way back to the main room to wait for the alarm to go off, which it did three minutes later.

Obviously, a fire was the least expected event because when the alarm did go off, no one knew what to do initially and there was just a lot of panic and milling around, shouting and confusion. In that melee, Hannah edged her way towards a fire extinguisher which was located on the wall between the cabinet and the door to the toilet area. It dispensed powder rather than water; a fact she had previously checked because only by discharging nine kilos of powder into the room, would it serve her purpose ... and she did, adding to the panic as now visibility was reduced. In that crucial thirty seconds, she hurled the spent extinguisher into the display cabinet, smashing it to smithereens. She whipped out the chalice; the powder in the air effectively masking her actions, particularly from the security cameras. She didn't take the chalice but lobbed it behind the counter of the gift shop where there were at least twenty others, then she dashed out and milled around with everyone else, coughing and spluttering. It wasn't difficult to edge away and disappear before more security, the pompiers and gendarmes turned up.

Why was all this necessary? To flush out the original chalice.

If a copy was indeed on display, then there was no possibility that the chalice would be a 'no show' the following day, and given the timing of Hannah's escapade there was very little chance that a new display case would be available with the same security as the original. Hannah was hoping that she had weakened the system sufficiently to provide an opportunity the following evening to swipe the cup - the original cup for that matter.

The following morning, she went back to the public viewing room to see how the land lay; a chalice was on display in a hastily installed cabinet. Was it the original? She couldn't tell but her goal was easier to accomplish. She went to the gift shop and purchased a replica, asking the sweet young thing for the one that wasn't boxed.

"It's a little dusty," admitted the girl.

"It doesn't matter; it makes it look older," said Hannah, smiling, and for two hundred francs she purchased *the* copy of the chalice and had secured herself eight hundred thousand francs in the process. The original was still her object but now there was less pressure.

She was also convinced that she had the copy because the theft the day before had not been reported; merely the fire had made the newspaper and that had been played down. If the original had been stolen, then she was sure that the matter would have been dealt with very differently.

Chapter Four – The Masquerade

On Saturday morning, Hannah danced and read the newspapers, and, after lunch, she packed up her things into two very smart cases and took them to Montparnasse Station where she left them in a left luggage locker. She returned to the room to change into her waitress's uniform, and she stowed the court jester costume for the ball in a small nylon holdall. In the room there remained the copy of the chalice, her travel clothes and bare necessities for her 'toilette'.

She had demanded that the handover be on the Sunday because the receptionist would be off, and the office downstairs would be deserted. She had purchased her railway ticket when she had stowed the bags in the locker. All she needed was the bearer bond and the fake IDs from Boehme.

With plenty of time, she made her way to the Fayette residence and checked in for duty, putting the small holdall under the bar counter. She stocked shelves and polished glasses, sharing the banter with her colleagues and generally blending in as far as she could. She had dressed her hair very plainly; simply tying it back and she wore her 'glasses' which had clear glass lenses. It was all designed to make her appearance unremarkable and forgettable.

At eight-thirty, the bar manager asked her to fetch more champagne flutes from the stock room which was reached along a corridor from behind the bar area. At that end of the corridor there was a door which led into the public viewing area. She tried the door and found it to be unlocked. Peering in, she saw no one on duty and the cabinet was now unlit but the security cameras still displayed their tell-tale red lights. A room on the right just before the end of the corridor held the security systems and that door was also unlocked and slightly ajar, but the room was manned by a security guard who was watching the CCTV monitors which covered almost the entire house. She fetched the flutes and got ready for the beginning of the ball. Guests were already starting to arrive; musicians were warming up and waiters began to ferry champagne out into the main area for the first arrivals. The Fayette's were all there, dressed in the most magnificent costumes, and by the look of it, adorned with most of the family heirlooms! It kept attention firmly in their quarter and well away from the bar.

Boehme had no idea what costume she was wearing to the ball, but she knew what he was planning to wear. The receipt for the hire of his costume had been on the receptionist's desk when she had visited him on Wednesday. It said, as best could be translated, 'black and gold highwayman outfit'.

"How appropriate," she had said to herself and at nine-thirty she spied him as he entered, looking like a cross between *Adam Ant* and *Louis the Sun King*.

She worked solidly, keeping her eye on him and watched him as he searched for her. At first, he just scanned the room then he entered into idle chit-chat with a few women. He was beginning to get frustrated she thought and judged it nearly time for her to join the party. She took her bag from under the counter and dived into the corridor, placing the bag in the stock room from where she had retrieved a bottle of champagne and a flute. She opened the bottle and poured a glass and then emptied the powdered contents of about five sleeping capsules into the liquid. She knocked on the door of the security room and the security guard opened it.

"Philip says this is with the compliments of the bar manager," she said in something approaching *verlan*.

He took the glass and the bottle, saying something crude which she just smiled at, and then she left, diving into the stock room again to change into her costume, stowing her uniform in the bag which she left there. She re-entered the corridor and checked on the security guard who was now pleasantly dozing in his seat. She turned off all the cameras and made her way into the public viewing area, picking up a replica chalice from the gift shop. No one was in the room and the new cabinet was much less secure than the old one. She was able to open the lock with her nail file, taking out the chalice and replacing it with the replica. She returned to the security room and turned the cameras back on. She put the chalice in the bag with her uniform and then headed into the party. Her only entry point was the bar itself, but she figured by now no one was going to care or probably notice as the gala was in full swing.

She picked up three lemons on her return and started to juggle them as she entered the bar, and her impromptu performance allowed her to get away with it. As far as the bar staff were concerned the 'jester' was probably hired for the occasion and they just played along, catching the lemons as she lobbed them in their direction.

She made it out onto the main floor and quickly found Boehme in the crowd who, even behind his mask, was looking pretty sullen. She tiptoed up to him and presented him with a silk flower which she pulled from out of the arm of the costume. He accepted it and he offered her his hand and they made their way to the dance floor and waltzed for the next ten minutes. He went off to grab them some drinks and she made her way out into the inner courtyard to smoke a cigarette.

When he found her, he said, "I had almost given up hope that you would come."

"I wouldn't have let you down. I had to attend to some business beforehand; it took a little longer than expected ..."

"Did you conclude your business?"

"Oh yes; everything's in the bag now ... Are we still meeting tomorrow?"

"Yes, at ten o'clock at the office as arranged," he replied.

"I have a surprise for you," Hannah said.

"Generally, I don't like surprises, but I feel sure I am going to enjoy this one."

"You will ... Shall we dance some more?"

They danced again but Hannah was in demand and soon lost in the crowd. When she judged the moment to be right, she left the floor and headed back to the bar, pulling more flowers out of her costume for the girls working there and she disappeared again into the stock room, changing quickly, returning to the bar and managing to hide her bag before anyone was the wiser. She worked on until two in the morning. Receiving her pay, she left and took a taxi back to the room in Montmartre.

Chapter Five – Pay off

She left the room spotless and grabbed a coffee in Rue des Abbesses before heading to the Le Marais and Boehme's office. The court jester outfit and the waitress's uniform found their way into a clothing bank en route, and in Hannah's holdall were the two chalices, the original and the copy. She arrived at the office and rang the bell because the door was closed. Boehme appeared at the door and let her in, escorting her upstairs.

"You left the Ball without saying goodnight," he said a little piqued.

"You wanted a surprise, didn't you?"

"Yes ... may I see it?"

"Do you have the bond and the IDs?"

He withdrew both from his desk drawer and placed them on his desk in front of her.

"As agreed ..."

She unzipped the holdall and pulled out one of the chalices.

"As agreed," she replied, inwardly smiling as she handed it over, scooping up the bond and the IDs, and putting them in her bag.

"And the surprise?" he asked, looking quite childlike.

She withdrew the other chalice and placed it on his desk.

"The original *and* the copy ..."

"How ...?"

"Don't ask," she replied, "and in return, I want the name of your associate from whom you obtain the IDs and the name of someone I can apply to for work ... if you follow me."

He eyed her intently for a full minute.

"I have to admit that I did not expect you to accomplish the task. In my wildest dreams did I dare to imagine you might get the original ... but both; that is very impressive. I will give you the name of the associate from whom I obtain the IDs ... as to a prospective employer, I'm not sure I want you to work again. There are other ways to make a living ..."

"Your concern is touching but if you thought we had a future then you are mistaken; I will be no one's mistress ..."

"Would you consent to be my wife?"

"If you weren't already married, Boehme, I might."

He sat back and smiled.

"My receptionist told you, didn't she?"

"One should be more careful with the things you entrust your receptionist to keep in her desk drawer; particularly when she fails to lock it when she goes to lunch ..."

"Ah ..."

"Insurance, Boehme; in case you felt the urge to become 'honest' in your dealings, particularly our dealings ... the names please ..."

Boehme wrote two names on a piece of paper and handed it to her. She put it in her bag and got up.

"Goodbye, Boehme; a million thanks."

"Goodbye, Mademoiselle; until the next time."

Hannah left and walked smartly in the direction of *Châtelet* and grabbed a Metro to Montparnasse. Within the hour, she had boarded her train for the South. In her view, a little holiday was called for whilst she contemplated her options and the small fortune she carried in her bag.

Crime Three - Rites of Passage

Chapter One – High Tide

Flushed from her dance class, Hannah sat down at one of the tables at her favourite café; the one on the harbourside, and watched the yachts gently sway on the incoming tide. She was "holidaying" in Saint Tropez and feeling quite relaxed; then she did have somewhere in the region of 1.4 million francs.

Unsure of just how dishonest Boehme was, she'd ditched the fake IDs he had obtained for her and had purchased new ones, directly from the associate who worked out of *Nice*. Not having paid for the ones which Boehme had obtained for her, they represented no loss. This was something she was beginning to understand better, this trading account in crime.

Hannah guessed, rightly, that Boehme both admired her confidence and was jealous of it. Only the threat to expose some of his secrets kept him from giving the names on the fake IDs to his friend at the police headquarters. She didn't trust him and had dumped the fake IDs, promising herself that she would avoid "go-betweens" in the future; they had the least amount to lose in her opinion. It also reminded her that this was no game. The career - if that was the right word - provided the adrenalin rushes she craved. In some respects, the money was a bonus, especially now.

Hannah's strengths lay in her impeccable memory and in her confidence. She also saw things which others didn't, and made acquiring skills and picking up information, habits of a second nature, spending three hours a day scouring the international press. Attended classes and perfected her disguises, the daily *pain beurre.*

When she got up in the morning, it could very well be that she said, "Today, I am a German student" or "an English teacher" or "a Spanish journalist", and for the whole day, she would live and breathe the persona.

Rigorous study was resulting in exceptional language skills; she spoke English and French like a native, German and Spanish to an advanced level, and Japanese and Russian to an acceptable level. She could make herself look twenty years older and looked just as comfortable in *haute couture* as she did in *M&S* off the peg. Dancing and working out sought to counteract the terrible habit of smoking twenty cigarettes a day.

Hannah had arrived in *Saint Tropez* in late August. The season was dying a little and it had been easier to find a room than she had expected. A car allowed her to drive frequently to *Nice* and occasionally to *Toulon* and *Marseille*. Itching to test all of her skills, she had decided that she'd needed a job that sealed her reputation as a professional thief of priceless art treasures.

Her choice of café seat had been deliberate; it gave her full view of the yacht *Aristotle*, owned by the German industrialist *Gerhardt*. He was currently hosting a lunch party for some close friends. After half an hour, Hannah left the café and made her way to a gallery in town where she had a "friend"; they took lunch together. The young woman was in Hannah's dance class and Hannah had made Sophie's acquaintance pretty quickly after she had found out where Sophie worked.

To Sophie, Hannah was *Madeleine* or *Maddy*.

"Sophie; I need your advice." Hannah opened up the conversation at lunch.

"What is it, Maddy?"

"I want to buy a painting, something of an investment for the future."

"I have just the painting for you ..."

They lunched and all the while, without making it obvious, Hannah pummelled Sophie for information about up-and-coming artists, local collectors, how the gallery business worked and who was spending the real money. In return, she gave away very little but did an excellent job of turning a few bare facts into a colourful tapestry. Sophie was a little awed by her and sat basking in the glow. They left and went back to the gallery to see the picture which Sophie had suggested might be the ideal investment.

"It is a minor work but that is also reflected in the price. All the major works are being snapped up by the Japanese banks and it won't be long before the minor works see their value ... in the end, there simply won't be anything else left to buy."

Hannah was standing before a *Paul Scholar*, a minor Impressionist painter from Holland. The piece was a self-portrait and about the size of a large cornflake's packet.

"His major works have begun to attract a lot of interest. I would say that soon you could not buy this for less than two hundred and fifty thousand francs. At one hundred and fifty thousand francs, it is a real bargain ... and if you promise not to tell anyone, especially the owner, I can tell you that the gentleman moored in the harbour, Gerhardt, is *very* interested ..."

"Is he? It would be a sound investment and I simply adore the Impressionists; I'll take it!" said Hannah with real joy in her voice; not that the picture was her object because Gerhardt was her quarry this time.

"If I sell it then I'll earn the commission too."

"Excellent! Where is Amelia?"

"*Marbella*, with Godfrey; due back at the weekend."

"I'll have the money on Friday; will you still leave it on display?"

"Oh yes; that's policy. But I can take it down if you prefer."

"No; leave it on display. Please don't sell it to anyone else ..."

Hannah left the gallery and skipped back to her room to fully hatch the plan. Her research thus far on the industrialist Gerhardt had been very illuminating; a self-made multi-millionaire, German by birth, married and divorced twice; currently wooing a French actress who lived in *Saint Tropez*. He owned the yacht *Aristotle* and had an extensive collection of Impressionist paintings, many of which were displayed on the yacht.

"I need an invitation to get aboard," she said to herself and started to practise her German while she memorised the auction prices of all of the lots in the last three Impressionist sales ... and painted her nails.

Chapter Two – Accidents will happen

Hannah drove a smart little Alfa Romeo *Spider,* bearing Liechtenstein plates. She owned the vehicle but under a different name to *Maddy* or Hannah, and it was registered to an address in Liechtenstein where her bank account was also registered. It had been one of those things which she'd always wanted, the Liechtenstein bank account. The bearer bond from Boehme for eight hundred thousand francs had been deposited in it as soon as she'd had the ID from Eckhart; the ID for a thirty year old Swiss National by the name of *Ruth Wald.* The car had been a prop at the time but she'd fallen in love with it so had bought it outright.

Two days after the lunch date with Sophie, Hannah dressed up in her chic *Saint Tropez* outfit - the white linen suit, fuchsia pink headscarf and very dark sunglasses - and drove the car down to the harbourside, timing her arrival with the departure of Gerhardt in his rather ostentatious *Maserati.* They pranged; a minor scrape which left a mark on her bumper and scratch on his front wing. He got out as did she.

"*Mademoiselle*; I believe *you* were at fault," he said peevishly.

Hannah dropped into her polished German and admonished him for his negligence and even suggested that he might have been eyeing something else rather than his bonnet. He laughed and practically slapped her on the back for her audacity in suggesting anything like it. He was a goat, shall we say and a little uncouth.

"If we call it even, how can I make it back into your good books?" he asked, eyeing her figure without any attempt to hide his lust.

"They say the *Aristotle* has an interior by *Versace*; I should like to see that," she said.

"Then come to dinner this evening ..."

"I accept."

"Come aboard at 7..."

"Thank you! I'm sorry but I have to run; I'm expected on board *Lady May* for lunch. Amelia has the prettiest *Paul Scholar* which she wants me to see."

"You know Amelia?"

"Yes; do you?"

"Not well; I've seen the *Paul Scholar*; a fine example. I was hoping to add it to my collection but the price is a little high for a minor work."

Hannah rattled off the prices of similar works from the last three auctions by way of establishing her credentials as a collector and suggested that the price could only go up.

"Let me know at dinner what you decided."

"At 7 then ..."

She sauntered off to the *Lady May* to accompany Sophie as her guest for lunch and both were expecting Amelia to announce her engagement to Godfrey ... and they were not disappointed.

Hannah confirmed her desire to purchase the *Scholar* and handed Sophie a cheque for the one hundred and fifty thousand francs.

"Gerhardt invited me to dinner this evening on board the *Aristotle*; shall I tell him I bought the picture?"

"How did you manage that?"

"He hit my car and felt duty bound to make amends for his carelessness."

"Perhaps he'll offer to buy the painting from you. He is due to lunch with Amelia on Monday, and she was sure he was going to make an offer for it."

"Let's see what happens ..." was all Hannah said in reply and they dined on lobster and paid Amelia all the compliments a ten carat engagement ring was duty bound to receive, silently mourning the probable loss of Godfrey's millions in the next divorce settlement.

Dressed *a la mode* and looking like *she* deserved to be wearing an engagement ring of quail egg proportions, Hannah arrived at the *Aristotle* at ten minutes past seven that evening, and was welcomed aboard by Gerhardt. He was dressed as *Captain Birdseye* thought Hannah secretly and her silent mirth illuminated her face so that even the goat put a leash on his tongue in the presence of a real beauty. He paid her a rather sweet compliment and she elevated him out of *uncouth* and into *unrefined*.

She accepted the glass of champagne which a steward brought on a tray, and they watched the sun sink towards the horizon.

"Did you enjoy your lunch?"

"Immensely *and* I purchased the *Scholar*. It is a sure-fire winner after the results of the next sale ... I expect to turn a handsome profit by the end of the year."

"If you sell, *please* give me first refusal," he pleaded.

"I agree; but first you owe me a tour of the interior ..."

He held out his arm and began his diatribe into the fitting out of the yacht and the cost of everything. Hannah murmured appreciatively in all the right places and memorised every single one of the paintings displayed on the walls. They dined by candlelight, and for the second time that day, she enjoyed lobster!

Chapter Three – Fish fingers, chips and peas

Hannah spent Sunday thinking very hard; she was at a turning point. Events over the past year had proved to her that she had a gift and, whereas the theft of the *Degas* had been more opportunistic and largely without an exterior motive, the *acquisition* of the chalice for Boehme had certainly been pre-meditated once she'd overheard his conversation on the telephone that day.

The name of the prospective *employer*, which Boehme had given her, along with Eckhart's, was the name of a very serious criminal and one she knew it would not pay to play games with. If she was to embark on this career, then this man was the type of person she would have to deal with, and it increased the stakes of the games exponentially. Confidence she had in spades, and some experience, but it was beginning to feel like tightrope walking over the Niagara Falls without a safety net.

If she pulled off the job this time, she promised herself a period of *retirement*. The theft of the *Degas* had not been reported to the police; the theft of the chalice most certainly had made the headlines. This latest *commission*, as she liked to call it, would put her on a *wanted list* for sure. But it would also earn her kudos; invaluable in getting herself more work, if she wanted it, and considerably larger fees.

Gerhardt owned five major Impressionist pieces, and all were on the yacht: she'd seen them, in the dimly lit library, during her tour.

Her commission was to steal all five, with handover in *Cannes*; the fee, two million francs. The theft of the chalice had convinced the client that she was capable. Merely thinking about it gave her a cold, sick feeling in the pit of her stomach.

"I can do this!" she repeated to herself as a mantra as she worked out the finer details of the plan. Getting back on board was easy now; leaving with five paintings, a little more difficult. Sophie came to her rescue in the most unexpected way.

"Amelia wants to put on an exhibition and raise money for the Red Cross; she's asked Gerhardt to loan his collection and she would like you to loan the *Scholar* for the evening. Please say you will."

"Of course I will; especially if Gerhardt is there."

"Are you angling for a proposal?"

"Heavens no! I want him to see the *Scholar* and be reminded that his hesitation has cost him a hundred thousand francs ... maybe more."

"Will you sell it to him?"

"No; not yet at least. Maybe after the next sale when the estimated value will approach five hundred thousand. When is the exhibition?"

"On Friday; from six until nine."

"There's no point taking the *Scholar* away for five days; keep it at the gallery until after the exhibition ... Amelia's engagement party is on Saturday, isn't it?"

"Yes; we must get outfits."

"Come with me to *Nice* tomorrow and we'll shop."

On Tuesday, they drove to *Nice* and purchased outfits; Hannah paid for Sophie's.

"Why, Maddy? I've already earned my commission on the *Scholar* thanks to you."

"For being such a good friend *and* for putting the *Scholar* my way; I'll make a fortune out of it in the end."

On Wednesday, Hannah researched the paintings which Gerhardt owned. The thing she wanted to know most of all were the paintings' dimensions. She got those from auction records and hoped he hadn't had them reframed. She bought five Impressionist prints; good quality ones, printed on canvas, and had them mounted on thin, light-weight insulation board. On Thursday, she took the prints, secreted in a portfolio bag, to the gallery on the pretence that she would collect the *Scholar* in it on the Saturday after the gala.

On Friday, she met Gerhardt for coffee in the harbour.

"Are you taking the actress to the engagement party tomorrow?" she asked, without batting an eye.

"That was my intention, yes; why do you ask?"

"No reason ... when are the pictures coming back on board; are you using a security firm?"

"This evening, after the show; I trust my security more than Amelia's."

"The *Scholar* is at the gallery and I don't want to take it home tonight after the exhibition; the flat will still be in turmoil following redecorating. Can you collect it with yours and I'll collect it from here on Saturday morning?"

"Of course; I'm staying off the boat on Friday night but I'll be back by ten-thirty on Saturday."

"Perfect; thank you."

Hannah left and went back to sort out the flat and make her preparations for the evening. The handover was on Sunday at noon in *Cannes* in the car park of the airport. It worried her a little that she would be carrying the paintings and would be alone. If the person or the people to whom she was handing over had a mind, they could easily wrest them from her, and she wouldn't be able to do a thing about it. But she hated involving anyone else; especially as there was an untraceable bearer bond for two million francs to think about.

At lunch on Friday, she cooked fish fingers, chips and peas and drowned the lot in tomato ketchup. The flaky pieces of meaty cod did wonders for her brain function that afternoon.

Chapter Four – The Exhibition

Hannah arrived at the gallery early to see Sophie and to give her a hand organising the caterers; also to make sure that everything looked perfect. All of the town's glitz was expected, if only to see Gerhardt and his girlfriend of the moment. Amelia didn't mind if it took attention away from her diamond; her party the following evening was expected to be graced by royalty. Godfrey couldn't put a foot wrong ... yet!

The exhibition was very light-hearted and well-attended but never very busy until eight o'clock. Then, everyone popped in to see the pictures, made a donation and hot-footed it to dinner; it meant not having to change. Hannah helped Sophie and Amelia butter everyone up. Gerhardt was talking to Godfrey and apparently, they were discussing the prospects for golf on Sunday - they were in fact talking prenuptial agreements and the respective charges of their lawyers. The actress girlfriend looked bored, and after thirty minutes, signalled that she wanted to leave. Gerhardt made a great show of leaving his donation and then left with the potential *trophy*. Hannah knew that the security firm was coming to collect the paintings at nine-thirty, and she offered to stay and help clear up after the show so that Godfrey could take Amelia out on a moonlit cruise.

"Darling; you're an angel. We have to sail with the tide; I will see you tomorrow at the party."

Amelia left at ten minutes past nine and at nine-fifteen, only Hannah and Sophie remained.

"Sophie; I'll pack the *Scholar* and put it with Gerhardt's; it's going back to the yacht with his. I'm picking it up from there tomorrow; quite possibly negotiating the re-sale, depending on the results of the auction this evening in Geneva."

"I'll be with you in a minute!" called Sophie from the back stockroom.

Quickly and expertly, Hannah removed the five prints she had purchased and fixed one over the top of each of Gerhardt's paintings using a safe, adhesive putty under each corner. They weren't a bad fit. She put them in the transport case and lastly put in the *Scholar* just as Sophie made her appearance.

"Oh Maddy, thank you! I really need to go soon."

"Is Jacques picking you up?"

"Yes; and you know how he hates to wait."

The security firm arrived and picked up the case.

"Great! All done," announced Sophie, flicking off the lights, adding, "the rest can wait until the morning."

The girls left and Hannah went back to the flat to finalise her packing and the arrangements for the handover on Sunday.

Chapter Five – Bon Voyage

On Saturday morning, at ten o'clock, Hannah went down to the harbour and went aboard Aristotle to wait for Gerhardt. The crew knew her and no one questioned her as she went to the main stateroom. A steward brought her a coffee and she waited patiently. Gerhardt arrived at ten-forty, in a filthy temper.

"She will drive me to insanity!" he flung out, only then noticing Hannah.

"*Mademoiselle*!" he added in better humour.

"What is it, Gerhardt?"

"She insists on … oh, what does it matter? Where are the paintings?"

"In the library, I presume; grab a coffee and I'll fetch the *Scholar* and maybe I'll make you a little happier," she said with a pretty little smile and Gerhardt threw himself into a chair and barked an order at the attendant steward.

Hannah came back with the *Scholar*.

"Remain calm, Gerhardt; it's nothing that can't be resolved in fifteen minutes … the security firm has picked up the wrong case-"

"What?" he bellowed and he tramped heavily to the library to see for himself that the case contained five different paintings, and in the dim light, he didn't notice the fact that they were prints and mounted in identical frames to his own.

"I'll take them back for you, Gerhardt, and I'll return with yours straightaway; there's no point calling the security firm because they'll be an hour getting here in the traffic. Relax, and whilst I'm gone, why don't you think about the *Scholar* and how much you are willing to pay for it. I won't fleece you *too* badly, but the results of the auction last night make for very impressive reading."

"Would you mind? I don't think I can cope with it. Tell Amelia I am very unhappy!"

"Of course, darling."

One of the stewards assisted her with putting the travel case, containing the six pictures, in the boot of the car as Gerhardt looked on.

"See you in half an hour!" he called out from the deck and waved.

Hannah waved back and drove off.

She called into the flat and picked up her two cases and then headed for the gallery to see Sophie.

"Sophie; I have to go to *Nice*; they put the wrong size dress in the bag. I'll be back by four o'clock."

"Don't be late because we're having our nails done at four-thirty."

"I won't; by the way, this is for you. It's a surprise for your birthday next week; don't open it until the day."

Hannah handed her the *Scholar*, with good title, wrapped securely and bedecked with a fuchsia pink bow.

"See you later," Hannah said and kissed her very tenderly on both cheeks.

She drove off.

An hour later, well clear of the storm that had suddenly erupted in *Saint Tropez*, she rendezvoused with the security firm at their offices in *Toulon* and handed over the case containing the five paintings.

"Tomorrow, at the airport car park in *Cannes*; eleven-thirty and *please* don't be late."

Were her instructions and she drove to *Cannes* and checked into the *Hotel de France* for the evening to study the newspapers and plan her *retirement*. She wondered if Gerhardt was angrier at the loss of his paintings or the fact that the *Scholar* she had left him with was a photograph.

Chapter Six – Hand over

At eleven the following morning, Hannah was stationed in the car park, awaiting the arrival of the security firm. They arrived at eleven-thirty, and she spoke to the two security guards, handing them sizeable wads of notes: all nodded.

At five minutes to twelve, a black *Mercedes* pulled up and two men got out. Hannah approached them with one of the security guards beside her.

"They're in the van," she said calmly.

The men looked at each other and Hannah knew, that had she been alone, the outcome of the meeting would have been very different. It had played out very well to have listened to her fears.

"Do you have the bond?" she asked.

One of the men handed over an envelope and she took it, glancing briefly to see that the precious contents were inside. She signalled to the other guard to remove the case from the van and hand it over.

"*Manuel* sends his regards," said one of the men.

Hannah just smiled and, once the case was in the boot of the *Mercedes*, she returned to the van with one of the security men, picking up her suitcases en route. The other security man got into her car and drove off. She remained in the van with the security guard until the *Mercedes* had disappeared.

"Thank you," she said to the guard.

"No problem; do you want me to escort you to the terminal?"

"No; that's fine. I'll be in touch," she said, and she left the van and headed into the airport terminal building to catch a flight to London.

Epilogue

"Mother; are you there?"

"Hannah?! How did you ... what?"

"I'm long overdue a holiday and I haven't seen you for ages," replied Hannah as she was crushed to her mother's bosom, receiving the hugs of all hugs.

"Your father will be so pleased to see you; you're looking peeky child ..."

Crime Four - The Nizza

Chapter One – Choices

Hannah's self-imposed retirement lasted for three years. Time enough for most people to forget most things. Not that she spent all three of those years on the Island with her parents; just the first. She let her Saint Tropez blonde locks grow out and put on the five kilos she'd lost as part of that "adventure", losing her gauntness, much to her mother's satisfaction.

Much to her father's satisfaction, she got a job in the library and bought a small flat near her parents' house in Ventnor. Her father introduced her to his bank manager for the purposes of applying for a mortgage. She thanked him and secretly paid for the flat outright in cash. She danced, and to all intents and purposes, looked like she might be settling down, and possibly getting ready for her first serious relationship, or so her mother prayed. Hannah had other ideas.

After a year, she fabricated a job offer in London, rented out the flat, packed her two smart cases, and said her tearful goodbyes. She spent a month in London, sorting out new IDs, and on her twentieth birthday, she flew to New York as *Sadie Goldberg*, an American student at Columbia University, studying art history.

She spent the next year studying, sometimes art but also a range of other subjects that now included computing. She rented a tidy little apartment on West 80th Street and worked part-time in one of the bookstores in the area of the University. Her fortune of three million French francs had converted to five hundred thousand US dollars. She still had her account in Liechtenstein; the car was in storage.

The third year of her retirement, which began on her twenty-first birthday and ended on her twenty-second, was spent travelling a little. Now there were choices to be made.

She didn't want to work for people like Manuel. He was a dangerous criminal and ruthless. Hannah never really saw herself as a criminal like him; she had class and never stole things that people couldn't afford to lose ... or so she judged.

Hettie hadn't lost anything except a fake *Degas* and a pretty lipstick case. Rathbone had gotten his soulmate. The Fayette's probably had the real chalice tucked away in a vault somewhere to one day be repatriated - replicas were still on sale in the gift shop. Gerhardt lost infinitely more after his messy divorce from the starlet, and he deserved it for his roguish manners. Therefore, Hannah's conscience was pretty clean, and her sleep remained untroubled.

She danced but was getting "bored", and that drove her to find a new employer. Skills needed to be used, or they became rusty, and after three years, her kudos was on the wane. It was high time she worked again.

She went to a gallery on West 23rd Street and stood in front of a *Pollock* with one of the arms of her sunglasses carefully placed between her perfect teeth.

"It's a fine example of his work," said the man at her side; not an employee but another customer.

She turned and, in a heavy Italian accent, purred, "I prefer sculpture; more animated; more real; more sensuous."

"So why are you looking at the Pollock so intently?" he asked.

She smiled.

"Sometimes it does to have a change ..."

She left, and he remained looking at the *Pollock* as if he was trying to see something in it which he had missed; something she had seen, undiscovered by anyone else.

"May I help you, Sir?" asked the gallery assistant.

"Do you know that woman's name?"

"*Signorina Fiorina de Cana*, I believe," replied the young man.

"Thank you," the man murmured, and then he left.

oOo

Hannah loved fishing, and to catch a fish such as Michael Burlington on the first excursion, was a real triumph. She had made her name known to the gallery assistant on one previous visit and hoped he had remembered it for she was sure that Michael would ask.

Back at the apartment, she returned to a magazine that she had picked up, which featured the Park Avenue apartment of Michael Burlington, and the exquisite bronzes he had acquired over the last ten years - one in particular, *The Muses* by *Adolfo de Nizza*.

The impetus had been a call from her friend Pierre, the security guard. Someone had contacted him, asking if he knew of her whereabouts. He had, as instructed, feigned ignorance but passed on the details of the enquiry to Hannah. Only Manuel would have known that the security guard had contact with her in the past. Manual was very well connected, and he had referred her, seemingly, to this person who had spoken to the security guard, leaving a number 'should the lady ever be in contact again'.

Pierre had followed the established protocol and had contacted Hannah a few days later.

"Maddy; it's Pierre. Contact was made the day before yesterday; an associate of Manuel I gather. His name is *Thierry Silber*. He gave me a number to call should 'the lady ever be in contact again' ... How do you want to play it?"

"I'll call you in a couple of days, Pierre; after I've found out what I can about him. I need to think this through carefully. If he's an associate of Manuel, then perhaps I don't want to know, and you're three thousand miles away this time. I'll get back to you very soon; thank you. Has everything been working properly with the transfers to your account?"

"Yes, Maddy; absolutely fine. I feel a fraud for taking the money and not doing anything for it."

"If I contact Thierry Silber, then he will know that you were in contact with me. That puts you back in the picture. If you'd prefer to stay out of it, then just say so; we don't know how dangerous this man is. Think about it and we'll talk in a few days; take care."

"You too ..."

Hannah needed to think seriously and delve to find out what she could about this man Thierry Silber. That would require a little subterfuge on her part.

That evening, before putting any wheels in motion, she sat and thought very hard about the future.

The buzz of getting into the game again could not be ignored; she missed it. The last three years had been necessary to acquire a new level of confidence and to learn as much as possible. Age played no part in this; she could be any age between eighteen and thirty-eight given an hour in front of the mirror. She had confidence and saw connections and solutions well before anyone else. She lived comfortably and had security; the money was less of a consideration compared to achieving the goal. She needed a goal. The theft of Gerhardt's paintings had elevated her into a different league, and that "commission" had been offered to her by virtue of the theft of the chalice from the Fayette Residence. Where did this lead? How high could she rise? Doubtless there were jobs and rewards greater than that.

She concluded that, if it appeared that Thierry Silber was less dangerous than Manuel, then she would speak to him.

She slept on her choices and had a bad dream, waking at three in the morning, convinced that someone had been standing by her bed, looking down at her. In her later remembrance of the dream, she realized that the person hadn't been looking down on her in her bed; it had been her coffin.

Chapter Two – Thierry Silber

No standard searches had brought forth a scrap about Thierry Silber, and Hannah wondered if the name was real at all.

She did not have access to police records. She trawled auction reports to find a name and, in a pretty obscure sale at Sotheby's in Sussex, she found the name *Terence Silver*. He'd purchased a bronze, an *Adolfo de Nizza* the piece titled *The Head of Medusa*. The same man?

Conan Chalk owned the bronze he had purchased. It appeared, therefore, that Silver had merely acted as the go-between, Hannah guessed. She decided to call Conan and ask for Terence Silver's number on the pretense that she wished to employ him in the negotiation of a purchase. That would require her to adopt a disguise, one she had been cultivating for the last six months - *Signorina Fiorina de Cana*, an Italian heiress of thirty years of age, living in New York.

She called Conan and made her introductions.

"An associate suggested that Terence Silver would be the ideal candidate, but I have to confess that I do not know anything about him, Conan; would you recommend him?"

"Without hesitation! He is very experienced and professional; do you want his number?"

"Yes; that would be very helpful."

Conan gave her the number; a London number and Hannah called it, introducing herself to Terence Silver, emphasizing how highly Conan regarded him.

"I would be delighted to assist you, Signorina De Cana; especially if the piece is a bronze. I have a great deal of experience in the field."

"Let me call you back in a few days and we'll discuss it again."

She telephoned Pierre.

"Pierre, if you're willing to get involved, then I'm going to contact Thierry Silber."

"It's okay, Maddy; they can't get to you through me. Do you want the number he gave me?"

She took a few seconds to finally come to the decision.

"Yes; give me the number ..."

After she had been relayed by three handlers, she was given his number and, as she had guessed, the number was the same as Terence Silver's.

"Monsieur Silber; this is Madeleine ... you wished to speak to me?"

"Manuel gave me your name and you come highly recommended. I need you to steal a bronze - *The Muses* by *Adolfo di Nizza*. Currently owned by-"

"Michael Burlington."

"Quite so! You are well informed. My client is offering three hundred thousand dollars for the commission."

"Five hundred thousand."

"The piece is only worth-"

"Five-point-three million dollars. My fee is ten percent plus reasonable expenses; payment via untraceable bearer bond."

There was silence for a minute although Hannah had the pounding of her heart in her ears.

"My client will pay five hundred and thirty thousand dollars if the piece can be delivered before the end of September."

"Deal; how is the handover to be arranged?"

"The piece will be delivered to our representative in New York - a woman by the name of *Signorina Fiorina De Cana*. She will take custody of the piece and give you the bond; she is merely acting as a go-between and will be innocent of our arrangement."

"Understood; I will call when I have a date and time."

Hannah rang off and practically had kittens. How the hell did they intend to recruit Fiorina to act as a go-between? A little later, Conan Chalk telephoned.

"Fiorina; I wonder if you could do me a huge favour. You know how difficult it is to find someone you can trust these days. I have a bronze coming into New York, which needs to be looked after for a few days. Can you accept it and deal with the agent upon delivery? They need to be paid; you'll have a bond to give them."

"Conan; I would be delighted to assist you. Just let me know when the piece is arriving and the name of the agent."

If Conan was willing to have her look after the piece, then her disguise must have withstood some scrutiny for she couldn't imagine he would approach her without assurances. The thought that at a future point in time, she would have the fee *and* the bronze in her possession raised all kinds of possibilities.

It was time to make the acquaintance proper of Michael Burlington.

Chapter Three – Michael Burlington

Once Hannah as *Fiorina de Cana* had left the gallery, she had gone to the apartment and had sat down to gaze at the pictures of the bronzes again. They were etched in her memory now. The plan to steal *The Muses* needed some thought; his apartment building was heavily protected and there were cameras everywhere.

An apartment on West 80th Street did not figure for someone of her standing; a student, yes, but a young heiress, no. She needed to rent somewhere, and that was next on the list of things to do. Finding and meeting Michael again was easy; he was everywhere. A rich playboy with varied interests; she had no doubt that he would be on her trail!

The plan began to fill her mind much like an "etch a sketch" picture; lines began to appear. The first solid line was a sale of bronzes in a week's time. She was certain that Michael would be there. She intended to be there herself and buy one of the sculptures, outbidding him if possible. There was nothing Hannah liked more than getting her hook into the mouth of a big fish. That left a week to organize the new apartment, and she looked at one in Chelsea on West 23rd Street, opposite the Chelsea Hotel.

Installed in the apartment - well, appearing to be living in the apartment - she gave thought to the sale and the piece that she would bid for and snatch out of Michael's jaws just as he tasted victory. It had to be another *Adolfo de Nizza*, she surmised, else he probably wouldn't be interested. The piece in the sale was fortuitously a small piece, and the estimate was somewhere in the region of one hundred thousand dollars. She would venture that for a payoff five times as big, and the piece would only appreciate.

Hannah took out the usual insurance. She was always thinking nine levels in both directions and nine steps ahead; 'a Vulcan playing chess' her father always said.

She registered and received her bidding card at the new address, adding a little more to the *Fiorina de Cana* "personality capital" as she called it; that which you invested in the person to make the rest of world believe that they were real. A year enrolled at Columbia as Sadie Goldberg had been the investment there; a bright student, a loyal part-time employee at the bookstore ... interest accrued and accruing.

The auction was being held at Doyle's on the Upper East Side on the Friday evening, starting at 8pm.

Upon arrival, she saw Michael and he saw her. Naturally he came over.

"Signorina De Cana! What an unexpected pleasure," he said, kissing her fingertips. She knew he would have scoured the register to confirm that she planned to attend.

"Mr. Burlington-"

"Please! Call me Michael."

"Michael; it is a pleasure to see. Are you in a buying mood?"

"Perhaps; you?"

"Perhaps ..."

They moved to their respective corners and waited for the referee to start the first round. Neither batted an eye as a procession of mediocre bronzes made their way out; most failed to make their reserves. The *De Nizza* was in the next section. Things became livelier as the auctioneer announced the piece and asked for bidding to start at fifty thousand dollars which no one touched. In the end, the opening price was twenty thousand dollars. No one expected it to stay there.

Two or three other bidders were showing interest but nothing serious. Hannah bid eighty thousand to signal to Michael that she was serious. He bid ninety and then she a hundred. It was the first piece of the evening to break through the one hundred thousand barrier. Heads began to turn in Hannah's direction. They perhaps fancied they saw a black panther; she swathed in ink-black wool by *Emmanuelle Vesuvius*, wearing an insanely large emerald necklace that everyone assumed must be real.

"One hundred and ten ..."

It was Michael's bid. Hannah raised her card.

"One hundred and twenty ..."

Her limit was one hundred and fifty thousand dollars. Even if she didn't get the piece, she'd get Michael. But getting the piece would establish her credentials as a collector, and a collector with money; a more powerful cocktail, she believed. Imperative if she was going to get inside that apartment of his and her hands on the *De Nizza*.

"One hundred and thirty to you, Sir ... Thank you, Madam ... one hundred and forty to you ... One hundred and fifty to the gentleman ..."

There was silence now as everyone sensed that this could become a *battle royale*. Michael, perhaps assuming that one hundred and forty was her limit, offered one hundred and fifty to claim the piece without getting into a pointless bidding war for something that wasn't all that important.

"One hundred and sixty to the lady ..."

Hannah broke her limit to see his reaction. He had the mask of gentlemanly conduct on his face, but she could see the blood rising and knew he was up for the fight.

"One hundred and seventy to the gentleman ..."

He stole a glance and unleashed a quick smile as if he was unsheathing his rapier.

"One hundred and eighty ..."

"Two hundred thousand dollars!" Michael quickly countered, betraying something of his true nature. He glanced again into the twin black moons of her sunglasses.

"Two hundred and twenty-five thousand dollars."

"Sir, the bid is against you."

He looked at her, narrowing his eyes, wondering why she was engaging him so blatantly without any hope of ever getting her money back.

"Two hundred and fifty!"

And when invited to bid, Hannah shook her head.

She quit the room, but Michael followed her. "Signorina! Please wait," he called out, adding, once she had turned, "I hope you're not too disappointed."

"Not in the least, Michael; you paid more than twice the value."

"You bid two hundred and twenty-five thousand."

"To see how far you would go to get what you wanted or, more accurately, deny me what you thought that I wanted ... it's a pretty piece."

She turned away.

"I'll give it to you if you agree to have dinner with me ..."

She turned back and fingered her emerald necklace, pausing for ten seconds before responding.

"I will accept your invitation, Michael; on one condition; you show me *The Muses*. They say no one has seen it for ten years."

He paused for ten seconds.

"Okay; tomorrow. I'll send a car to pick you up at seven-thirty."

"I have my own car. I'll see you tomorrow at seven-thirty, and after you've shown me the piece, you can take me to dinner. Have tonight's *spoils* delivered to the gallery where we met."

She did leave this time and headed home to the 23rd Street apartment to make some calls. The first was to the gallery.

"Samuel; the *Adolfo* from tonight's sale will be delivered tomorrow. Sell as agreed: for three hundred thousand to the Californian ..."

The second call was to her favored driver.

"Pete; job tomorrow night. Pick me up at seven. Thank you, darling."

And the third call was to Pierre.

"Pierre; can you get here in two days? ... Excellent!"

Hannah crashed from the adrenalin burn and meditated with a scotch and a cigarette.

"So! Highly competitive - much as we expected ... but generous too. I wonder how generous he would be if he knew that *I* had sold the piece to him tonight, at a profit of one hundred and fifty thousand dollars, *and* three hundred more to come. Perhaps collecting and not stealing would be more lucrative - but so much less exciting!"

Hannah had purchased the piece just before the auction and had then re-entered it in the sale. The original seller had been more than happy with one hundred thousand dollars - perhaps less happy now.

"Four hundred and fifty thousand dollars ..." was Hannah's last thought as she slipped into bed.

Chapter Four – The Muses

Hannah dressed to kill; a backless, black, velvet dress and respectable rubies. Pete picked her up at seven o'clock to ferry her to the Park Avenue apartment of Michael Burlington.

"Where shall I collect you later?" he asked.

"At the *Gotham*; at around eleven-thirty."

"Enjoy your evening."

"Thanks, Pete."

She entered Michael's building, and the concierge called up to obtain authorization for the elevator to take her to the top floor.

"Top floor, Signorina," he announced, and she tipped him ten bucks.

Michael came out to welcome her. The lobby was clad in grey and white marble, lit by Baccarat crystal chandeliers.

"Signorina!"

"Please call me *Fiorina*, Michael; I think we're passed those formalities now, don't you?"

"Yes; please come in. May I offer you a drink?"

"Some champagne perhaps?"

"Are we celebrating?"

"The *De Nizza* makes a fine addition to my collection; that was uncommonly generous of you and very sporting. What time is our reservation at the *Gotham*?"

"How did you know that I'd booked the *Gotham?*"

"I called all of the restaurants in Manhattan."

"Why?"

"I generally don't like surprises. However, I'm prepared to make an exception in the case of *The Muses*. Why haven't you shown it in ten years?"

"I don't like sharing."

"So why did you give me the piece?"

"I like games and to dine with beautiful women."

"I would have said *yes* regardless."

"Where would the fun have been in that?"

"Quite!"

They sparred like regular heavyweights, but both held their punches.

"Do you still want to see it?" he asked as he handed her a glass of champagne.

"Yes ..." with just enough excitement in her voice to register genuine interest.

He escorted her through the apartment, which was just as it appeared in the magazine photographs. The space was opulent, and bleeding art from every surface; lit by Baccarat and decorated in mostly muted tones; white silk and grey satin, dried blood red suede and matt black leather. The piece was exhibited in a room all its own, which have once been the library or a study. The muses were life size. In this case, three in number, not nine - even three had required the floor to be reinforced. The group comprised representations of *Melete, Mneme* and *Aoide.*

Cast in bronze and worth 5.3 million dollars; Michael had purchased the piece ten years ago - and at two million dollars then, the highest price paid for any bronze cast in the last one hundred and fifty years.

Hannah toured the sculpture, walking around it twice, before coming to a standstill to sip her champagne and allow her gaze to rest on the piece. It hadn't been sculpted in the traditional style; it was more abstract and highly polished, like glass. Each figure flowing into the others, the spaces between them resembling the windows of the *Casa Mila* in Barcelona; organic and hypnotically simple. The light reflected off the highly polished surfaces to create a mesmerizing aura.

"Satisfied?" Michael asked quietly.

In the presence of real beauty, Hannah had momentarily lost her voice.

"Beautiful, Michael; you really should exhibit it ... It's too important to be shut away in this room."

"Like I said, I don't like sharing. It took five years to negotiate the deal to have the photographs taken."

"Why did you agree to show it to me?"

He grinned, a little embarrassed.

"I wondered if your beauty would stand up to it."

"Satisfied?" she thrust back.

"More than ... Shall we go to dinner?"

"Yes; thank you for the opportunity to see it in person."

They dined and skirted rather than flirted. Hannah had only agreed to dinner so that she could see the sculpture and the apartment. The rest bored her steadily to tears. Michael assumed she would fall into his arms; she didn't and that left a smear on the flawless performance.

"Can I offer you a ride home?" he asked.

"No, thank you; I have a car waiting."

"You are annoyingly independent."

"I'm a modern woman; I have my own money and my own business."

"What about love?"

"What about it?"

"Do you believe in it?"

"Of course ... on my terms."

"Which are?"

"An exhibition; show *The Muses* and the other pieces in the collection. When you've learned to share, then talk to me about love. Goodnight, Michael; thank you for dinner."

She left; a panther weaving its way through the tables. At the door, she blew him a kiss. Only when he got up to leave, did he find that she'd already paid the tab. Crucified; that's how he felt, and drawn to her like a moth to a flame.

Getting Michael to exhibit the piece was central to the plan to steal it; there was no other way. It was far too heavy to steal from the apartment, and it was impossible to evade the building's security with an object that large. As it was, it had been necessary to remove the doors when the piece had been installed. No; an exhibition was the only way, and the deadline of the end of September was just six weeks away.

Chapter Five – Criminally easy

"Fiorina; I will agree to show the pieces if you agree to share something too; share some time with me ..."

"We'll both need to see a little sign of faith; when I see the exhibition advertised, I will consent to a further evening with you. By the middle of September, the exhibition must open."

"Why by then?"

"I leave for Rome."

"You do?"

"Yes; I have business there."

"That's only four weeks."

"Time enough surely; everyone will be falling at your feet to host the event."

"Give me a week."

"Give me a copy of the event contract and I'll agree to spend the weekend with you."

"This is beginning to sound like business."

"Love is a serious business, Michael."

She rang off to let that gem sink in. It wasn't for the first time a man had become infatuated with her. She was shrewd enough to see them for what they truly were ... collectors of art.

"A woman I may be, but a trophy I am certainly not!" were her words to herself as she stretched her body before heading to her dance class.

In a week, she had the contract for the exhibition, having had it delivered to the 23rd Street apartment. Pierre was installed in the 80th, waiting for her instructions.

"Pierre; I have it. I'll meet you later and we can agree the details ... if you want in."

"Maddy; I'm in. It'll give me a chance to earn all that money you've paid me."

"You already did. The payoff from this will mean you can retire and keep out of harm's way."

The plan was refreshingly simple. Now that she knew where and when the piece would be moved, she would ensure that *her* security firm picked up the piece and delivered it to Thierry - while a replica of the piece was delivered to the exhibition hall; a replica good enough to fool everyone except Michael. No one else had actually seen it in the flesh for ten years. The entire operation was probably going to set her back two hundred thousand dollars *but* Michael had effectively paid for it himself; a thought which gave her a wicked little smile.

Now that the contract had been signed, she was duty bound to see through her side of the bargain; to spend a weekend with him. It was not something that she was relishing but the payoff was so big that she just buried her anxieties and began packing. She also called Thierry to confirm the date and time of the theft and the handover arrangements.

"Have the piece delivered to 255 Exterior Street in The Bronx and then inform *Signorina De Cana*. Once she has confirmed that the piece has been delivered, she will give you the bearer bond."

"Okay. Will she know it's stolen?"

"No; she's innocent in this - just the go-between."

A day or two later, Conan called to confirm the arrangements.

"The agent will inform you where the piece has been delivered to, and after you have confirmed that it is there, you can hand over the payment. On the morning of the delivery, the payment will be couriered to you."

"I understand perfectly, Conan; I'm happy to assist you."

Roughly three weeks remained before the exhibition. In those three weeks, the replica needed to be finished and a security van purchased and painted in the same livery as the firm that Michael was using. Pierre was doing that, now that they knew which firm was being used. Hannah saw to the replica. A student at the University had agreed to make the copy for her; not from bronze but using a new latex material stretched over a thin but strong wire framework; very light and reasonably cheap. The boy was infatuated with her but wasn't anything like as demanding as Michael.

The weekend approached and it couldn't be avoided; she just hoped he would be a gentleman. Could a weekend of playtime in Connecticut be all bad?

Chapter Six – La Fache

Michael picked her up and drove them to the farm he owned in Bridgewater, Connecticut; a 70-acre estate of mainly rolling grass and some mixed timber. There were a few horses, and the house had a fine view over the lake; it was stunning.

Staff unloaded the car, which allowed Michael to escort Hannah around the house, finally depositing her at the bedroom he had ordered to be prepared. Hannah, assuming they would be sharing from the off, was greatly relieved.

"Dinner is at eight o'clock; time to freshen up. Cocktails are at seven-thirty. Do you need anything?" Michael asked.

"No; I have everything I need; thank you, Michael. Game playing aside, I am looking forward to this weekend and the opportunity to get to know you better."

"Me too," he said with a genuine and soft smile, which perhaps even indicated that he was a little shy and maybe far less experienced in matters of the heart than most people would have guessed. He kissed her hand and left her at the entrance to the room. It had its own bathroom and a balcony with views over the rear formal garden and the lake beyond.

Hannah's bags had been brought up and she unpacked the essentials. She suddenly felt like a little girl in the grown-ups' world. This was her first taste of true style, and never before had she been entertained by someone with so much money - even Gerhardt's fortune paled by comparison.

A little awestruck, yes, she was, but she also processed everything. In particular, how certain things were done and arranged. Her etiquette was improving all the time. If she made a faux pas, and she did sometimes, she handed it off as youthful ignorance - but made damn sure she didn't make the same mistake again. In her current guise, she was thirty and travelled, wealthy and in business; it behooved a level of confidence and style. A level she wasn't used to yet but adapting to very quickly.

Something she did too was to watch herself, she did it all the time; stepping out of the body corporeal and floating above it to examine the performance for later analysis and agreement on points of improvement. Not knowing if the room was bugged or under surveillance, she acted out her persona unfalteringly. It was necessary anyway. She needed to wear the skin of Fiorina as closely as her own, and the heavily accented English was hard to maintain when she got into full flow. These trials, she mused, were what you got paid for. In reality, any idiot could steal a piece of art; getting away with it and advancing in the game was something else entirely.

She dressed chic and European. The black, knee-length dress accentuated her curves and her fluidity. Michael presented her with a corsage which was unexpected but earned him a kiss on the cheek and he beamed as if he believed that he had gotten something right. They had Cosmopolitans on the rear terrace and watched the sun set; clichéd as it was, it was very nice.

"If I may ask, what business interests do you have in Italy?" he asked. Hannah had been expecting the question after her reference to 'her business' the last time they had met.

"Fabric ... I trade in exquisite fabrics; mostly antique. I source most of it for designers and studios."

"I never imagined it could be so lucrative," Michael replied.

"It never was but the market has picked up in the last couple of years. There is a lot of new money and a desire to spend it conspicuously ..."

"Perhaps we can work on a project together; the apartment needs a make-over. Planning to move the bronzes just emphasizes how tired it looks. I haven't let anyone touch it for ten years."

"That suggests more than a reluctance to share your things."

"If I can be completely honest, I have no real confidence in these things; I buy the best and assume it will look amazing."

"Often it does but sometimes it can all work against you. I prefer simplicity. Good lighting, that's the key and that's my next business venture - lighting. The best designers are emerging from Sweden and Norway. Teamed with fabric, I believe I might have a winning combination."

"You are incredibly ambitious ..."

"For someone of my age; was that what you were going to say?"

"Actually, for a woman. You're spearheading an emerging confidence; I like it. It's refreshing ... you always seem younger than I know you are, but age is irrelevant."

"But experience is priceless and that can't be bought. I make it my business to acquire it; age doesn't matter until the client would prefer to deal with either a man, of any age, or someone with acumen. Fortunately, an increasing number of my clients are women, independent women; they care less about age or gender but drive harder bargains than the men!"

"Would you consider a partnership for the lighting venture?"

"I might; once I've seen how you do business."

"Ruthlessly as a rule; my world is inhabited by men ... who play golf and drink scotch."

"For now!" Hannah concluded; signaling that soon there would be no place to retreat.

They dined on simple farm-style fare cooked by a French chef and served by an English waiter. The wines were recommended by the chef and Hannah realized then that Michael had no real confidence. He bought the best and assumed it *would* look and presumably taste amazing. It did; but it wasn't very intimate, and more like dining in a restaurant in Paris or perhaps New York - although now that the *avant garde* had broken through, the stuffiness and formality of dining out was becoming more exciting and relaxed.

"Shall we take our coffees outside? The terrace is heated," Michael ventured.

"Yes; perfect."

Hannah wanted to smoke but asked first.

"Of course! I don't, well, cigars occasionally."

"It's a terrible habit," she admitted as she extracted a cigarette from her case and fitted it into the holder, allowing him to light it for her, using her newly acquired *Dunhill Rollagas*.

"What do you want to do tomorrow?" he prompted.

"Can we ride?" she asked, for she rode very well.

"Of course! Let's breakfast at eight and we'll ride before lunch. I want to show you the vineyard; it's just getting going ..."

It certainly wasn't expected, as far as Hannah could detect, that they would become intimate that evening. She kissed him very tenderly as she said goodnight and he responded in kind, holding her hand and then reluctantly letting it go as she moved to retire. He was thirty-eight, she recalled, as she took off her makeup, and he certainly didn't display the sexual confidence of a thirty-eight-year-old male. On one level, she wondered if he was indeed thirty-eight; perhaps he was twenty-two and masquerading like her.

That thought stuck in her head until she dropped off.

Chapter Seven – Huntin', shootin' and fishin'

Hacking across the downs on her native Isle of Wight had been one of her adolescent passions; hair streaming behind her and the wind making her eyes water. This was something that she didn't need to do better or practice. The four-year-old chestnut gelding relished being ridden and Hannah was in danger of falling into the island vernacular while she felt so free.

Michael battled bravely on his grey mare; an older horse and a pretty steady one. He didn't ride often or look at all comfortable, but he was competitive and pushed himself and the horse, until all pulled up breathless at the site of the new vineyard.

"You ride well!" he gasped.

"I love riding!"

He showed her the new vineyard. The vines were very young, and it would be a good few years before there was any *Chateau La Fache* on the shelves. They cantered back for lunch and then had a swim in the heated pool, followed by a game of croquet.

Hannah felt like she was being wooed in the good old-fashioned way and had to admit to enjoying it very much. They broke up after some tea for a siesta, planning to reconvene at dinner which was at seven- thirty. Hannah retired to a hot bath and Michael went to the office which was directly beneath her bathroom. His muffled voice was just audible as she soaked in the luxurious bubbles. Curiosity got the better of her in the end. She slipped out of the bath and took a glass from the shelf, placing the tumbler on the floor with her ear pressed to it to see if she could hear him more clearly. He was on the telephone.

"As far as I can see, Conan, she is who she says she is ..."

Hannah's heart skipped a beat.

"The exhibition was her idea, partly, I just don't see how the job gets done; the piece weighs two tons, man! I thought the other woman was the thief and our Italian friend was innocent ... oh, you think?"

"Oh my God," said Hannah to herself. "Conan is in on this and thinks *Madeleine* and *Fiorina* are the same person ... why ask for the piece to be stolen?"

"If they are, then she is very, very good. How do you want me to play it?"

Hannah strained to catch every word, seeing as this could be the end of her game or the start of a much bigger one.

"I won't do that, Conan; not for you or any amount of money. I'll cancel the exhibition. The piece is going nowhere and, as far as I'm concerned, she's innocent until proven guilty ... Remind me why we wanted the piece stolen in the first place? ... Don't threaten me!"

There was a long pause.

"Fine! We'll proceed as planned and see how she plays it; if I lose the piece, you'll answer for it - yes!"

Hannah got back into the bath and tried to remain perfectly calm. The burning question was why did they want the piece stolen? It was as if they were trying to flush her out. Could Gerhardt be behind it, seeking revenge? Manuel was happy - he had his paintings - so why the subterfuge?

Hannah went down for cocktails and played it very, very coolly; Michael appeared to be a little agitated.

"Is everything alright?" Hannah asked.

"Yes, fine; there's always some issue or other to sort out. The exhibition may have to be postponed ..."

There it was the test of her reaction.

"Now that *would* be a shame and you would be penalized by the venue ... but if the show is deferred, then I'll head to Rome earlier than planned. When will you know?" she asked as a matter of fact, and that floored him.

"Next week, by Wednesday," he replied somewhat meekly.

They dined and the atmosphere was a little heavy on Michael's side of the table; Hannah kept up the façade perfectly.

"If you have to delay, then come to Rome," she said as her own test.

"If it is possible, then I will; that would be great."

"What are our plans tomorrow?" she asked, keeping a toe in the water.

"I think we'll have to return to the city earlier than planned, perhaps after breakfast. Would you be very disappointed if we didn't go sailing?"

"Of course; but there will be other opportunities, won't there?"

"Yes, absolutely!"

They took their coffees and brandies out onto the terrace and Michael seemed more relaxed.

"You have been a delightful companion this weekend," he began. "There's a benefit on Tuesday which I have to attend; would you be my guest?"

"I *should* be free. I have an associate flying in for a meeting. Once I've checked the itinerary, then I'll confirm. It should be fine."

"If I said I needed your help, Fiorina, could I rely on your absolute discretion?"

"Of course, Michael; I'll do whatever I can to help."

"I've gotten into deep water and the raft has sprung a leak ..."

"Do you need money?"

"Ready money; I have so much tied up in other ventures. I don't want to pull the plug and lose out, *but* I have some heavy expenses coming in and even I have limits ... it would just be for a few weeks."

"How much?"

"Five hundred thousand dollars ..."

"That doesn't sound like too much of a problem. When do you need it?"

"By Wednesday as it happens."

"Okay; once I've seen my associate, then I'll see what I can do. Please don't worry, Michael."

"Thanks; I hate to ask but if I go elsewhere then-"

"Questions will be asked and that would be unhelpful."

"Exactly!"

"I'll be able to confirm on Tuesday, by the time I see you at the benefit. I'm touched actually that you trust me enough to confide in me and seek my help."

"You seem - no, you are - someone I feel I can trust. There are precious few; most just want to see me fail."

"Say no more about it. Where is the benefit on Tuesday?"

"At The Cloisters; it's in aid of a restoration project ... some tapestry or other."

"I've seen something about it. What time?"

"Seven; let me pick you up."

"I may be out. I'll meet you there, but you can drive me back. If it's early enough, there may be time to catch a late dinner."

"Thank you, Fiorina; I feel a lot easier about everything."

With a little haste, he retired and bade her goodnight very tenderly. Hannah remained on the terrace to think.

"He needs money; that's rubbish! So why say he does? To get five hundred thousand back for someone, perhaps to get the five hundred thousand to pay *Maddy* for the theft ... or see me broke ..."

She watched the full moon rise over the lake. As it inched higher into the sky and lit up the landscape, she had a few more thoughts.

"He's warning me - five hundred thousand is the payoff - it's just a scam to get half a million dollars, knowing that I won't be able to pursue it. It's their way of blowing my cover. Is it a test ... why? I could write it off but why should I? Does it buy me protection or seal my fate? Do I retire out of this game?"

Hannah went to bed and knew that the offensive would be her best defense, so she planned her own strategy.

They breakfasted and Michael confirmed that they needed to go back shortly afterwards.

"I'm really sorry," he said.

"It's fine; I'll do some work and that should almost guarantee that I'll be free on Tuesday evening. You can trust me, Michael, but I will need collateral for the loan," Hannah said, looking directly into those usually impenetrable pools of liquid flint. There was a ripple.

"No; of course ... What works for you?"

"If no one else must know, then personal assets to the value. You decide ..."

"I'll let you know on Tuesday."

They left and headed back to the city. The mood was fairly upbeat, which indicated to Hannah that Michael believed she would hand over the money, and she was pretty sure the collateral would be worthless. He dropped her off with a sweet little kiss and profuse thanks.

In the sanctuary of the apartment, she concluded that this was a cunning plan to oust her from the game; clear her out and send her packing, nursing her wounds. A simple case of removing the opposition before they became too powerful; suggesting Michael had more to lose than was apparent if she succeeded.

She waited until late afternoon and telephoned Conan.

"Conan; I hate to do this to you, but I have to fly back to Rome for business; it means I won't be here to handle your delivery."

"Is there no way you can be back in time, my dear?"

"It seems not. I hate to let you down and if you need someone you can trust, then I recommend Michael Burlington to you."

There was a pause.

"Yes, perhaps he would do it; we have had some dealings in the past. It's such a pity you can't do it; it would be an excellent way to forge a basis for future dealings."

"Such is life, Conan; goodbye ..."

All hinged on whether Thierry called *Maddy* but Hannah took the initiative there too.

"Thierry; it's Maddy. I've checked out the delivery address and it's unsafe; you'll need to advise me of an alternative ... Oh yes, the delivery will still be made ... Thank you; I'll wait for you to advise."

"That should put the proverbial cat amongst the pigeons *and* save the identity of *Signorina Fiorina de Cana*. Now, I wonder how Luke is getting on with the fake."

Such were Hannah's thought as she hatched a more devious plan to get her five hundred and thirty thousand dollars.

"Pierre; hi, it's me. Is the vehicle ready? Excellent! Meet me for lunch tomorrow; usual place, usual time."

Hunting and fishing and hopefully *no* shooting were Hannah's last thoughts as she got into bed. Who was behind it really? Conan? Michael? Thierry? She'd dismissed Gerhardt, having seen that he'd bought more paintings with the insurance money and was now courting a Duchess. The Fayette's didn't feature but she couldn't be sure. No, the plan had to have been concocted between Michael and Conan, with Thierry acting as a go-between, perhaps goaded by Manuel. She slept soundly and still held on to the feelings that, given a choice, she'd still rather steal than collect!

Chapter Eight – Reckoning up

On Monday, Hannah reconciled her accounts and found that if it were necessary, she could put up the five hundred thousand and it wouldn't make too much of a dent. She had about four hundred thousand from the sale of the small *De Nizza* which was bonus money; a hundred thousand from reserves would still leave her comfortable *but* she had no intention of seeing half a million dollars disappear without trace, and the damage to her reputation would effectively put her out of business.

Pierre had the vehicle ready and, in a day, or two, Luke would have the copy of *The Muses* completed for her to see. The plan was simple: load the copy into the security vehicle; drive to the delivery address; hand it over; collect the bond. The key: making sure that no one could verify that the real piece had not moved from the Park Avenue apartment. As long as Michael didn't oversee the handover, she'd be fine; he, therefore, needed to be elsewhere!

How to handle the benefit was the next burning question. Could she make it appear that she was handing over the money; would the collateral actually be worth anything? Did she back out, feigning heavy expenses of her own? Perhaps she should just leave for Rome like she had told Conan and leave the playboy with no playmate. Obviously, they thought relieving her of the cash would put an end to her career for a while; just to see her exit from the stage wasn't good enough.

The benefit for the tapestry was the key. She'd offer to pay Michael's donation instead of handing him the actual cash; that would delay matters. Perhaps she should sell the emeralds; they really weren't her. They were real but of very poor quality; the setting and the diamonds had hidden that fact. Worth a hundred thousand but looked a million. Yes, offer to cover his donation and sell the emeralds, put that money up and promise the rest a week or so later.

She wondered how Conan and Thierry would handle the bond and what had been said after her call to Thierry asking for another delivery address. She surmised that Michael was probably stepping up his security just in case.

On Tuesday, she called Thierry to get the address, feigning impatience as the plan was incomplete without it.

"I need the new delivery address, Thierry; by Friday, please."

"How do you plan to do it?"

"If I told you, you wouldn't need me, would you?" Hannah replied, laughing, also imagining the three of them scratching their heads, wondering how she planned to pull it off.

Michael's demeanor that evening would be interesting to say the least. It wouldn't matter if he stepped up the security; she would not be going anywhere near the place. But he needed to be put out of action and, if he was, who would they send to verify the piece before the bond was handed over? Her only advantage being that no one had seen the sculpture in the flesh for ten years and the fact that Luke was doing a painstaking job of making a copy. It was costing her thirty thousand dollars all told but worth every cent.

She got ready for the benefit, confirming with Michael that she would be arriving a little later than planned. Her proposal to pay his donation would be made at the last minute so that he didn't have a chance to say no. Playfully, she wore a pinstripe suit and a dress shirt of snowy white to really set off the rubies - which were fakes but exceedingly good ones, the fake pear-drop diamond earrings, her good watch and the trademark sunglasses. Pete dropped her off and she found Michael waiting in the foyer to escort her inside.

"Fiorina; you're dazzling tonight," he said, smiling broadly.

"Going out with a bang," she replied cryptically

"When do you fly?"

"Thursday, after my meetings ... Shall we go in?"

They went in and he grabbed them some champagne.

"Are you still confident that we can conclude our business before Thursday?" he asked in a very carefully chosen tone.

"Absolutely! And I have a wonderful idea; I'll cover your donation here tonight ... presumably that would have presented a problem to you as you need ready money, no?"

"I was going to make a fairly modest donation actually, which I could cover."

"You have a reputation, Michael. If they get a whiff of anything, then you'll have more issues to resolve, especially if they're also backing your projects. These things have a habit of knocking each other over. How much would they expect you to donate?"

"At least two hundred and fifty thousand."

"I'll cover that and let you have the other two hundred and fifty on Thursday; will that work for you?" she asked, smiling very sweetly, practically laying her heart open for inspection.

"That will work just fine. I'm so grateful, Fiorina ... as for the collateral-"

"Never mind about that, Michael; we're friends and I trust you will make good in the fullness of time ... it will be one less thing to worry about."

"It pains me to take advantage of your generosity, but I am exceedingly grateful."

"Say no more ..."

They mingled, together and separately. Hannah spoke to the event organizer and handed over a cheque for fifty thousand dollars on her own account and fifty thousand for Michael - effectively the proceeds from the sale of the emeralds. When the event organizer took the money, which they believed was from Michael, they raised an eyebrow.

"Darling; I hear things aren't going too well ... please don't mention it," Hannah pleaded in a very confidential tone.

"Signorina; we never disclose the details of how much an individual has donated."

"Excellent. As a dear friend, I wanted to spare him the embarrassment; these things can be judged very harshly, and the information could be damaging, shall we say."

She left the organizer and found Michael.

"It's done; don't worry about a thing and on Thursday, you'll have a draft for the balance."

"Thank you," he said. "Are we still on to catch dinner?"

"Yes; if you're free. My car is waiting; is yours?"

"I came with *Marco de Vron*; let's take yours. I have reservations at the *Metropolis*."

"Perfect! And I can tell you about the new venture. I'll leave you time and space to make your investment if you still want to once things sort themselves out."

They left and found the car. Pierre was driving, not Pete.

"Where to, Signorina?" he enquired.

"The *Metropolis*, please."

They headed off and Hannah kept Michael distracted with her tittle-tattle so that he didn't pay any attention to the journey or the route they were taking. It was only when his internal clock registered that he should be where he expected to be, that he looked out the window. He didn't recognize where he was.

"Hey! Where are we?" he demanded of the driver.

"Pete?" queried Hannah.

Pierre stopped the car and looked around.

"It's *Pierre*, madam." With which he shot a tranquilizer dart into Michael's chest, who slumped within a few seconds.

"Right; let's get moving!" urged Hannah.

Pierre had driven the car because he was roughly the same height and build as Michael. He swapped clothes with Michael, and they managed between them to haul Michael into the trunk of the car.

Hannah drove and took them back to Park Avenue where Pierre alighted, diving into the building. With his hat pulled down and his collar turned up, he avoided being recognized by the doorman and made it to the elevator where he used Michael's key to operate the elevator.

Hannah drove off and parked the car in the garage attached to her building, checking on Michael, who was out for the count.

"Goodnight, sweetheart!" she said as she entered her building from a side door.

She called Thierry.

"Change of plan, Thierry; the piece will be moved tomorrow, and I need that address!"

"There's a warehouse, corner of West 48th Street and 12th Avenue; be there at eleven o'clock in the morning."

"Who will take delivery?"

"I'll be there myself with the payment."

"Excellent!"

Hannah called Pierre at Michael's apartment.

"Delivery is at eleven o'clock in the morning; expect the call shortly afterwards."

"Okay, *Maddy*; good luck!"

Chapter Nine – Appearances can be deceptive

Early the following morning, after giving Michael another tranquilizer shot, Hannah took the security van and collected the copy of the sculpture from Luke. Between them, they easily lifted it *but* in order to fool anyone else, they secured the ensemble to a heavy base which was on a pallet, already in the back of the van.

"Thanks, Luke," Hannah said as she handed him thirty thousand dollars.

"Can I see you later?" he asked hopefully.

"Sure ..."

She went to Pete's place and picked him up; he was dressed as a security guard of the firm.

"Let's go!"

En route, Hannah changed into a uniform, also putting up her hair, donning a wig and fixing her makeup so that she looked Spanish. They arrived at the delivery address - a disused warehouse near the Chelsea Piers.

A car was already positioned just inside the door and a man was standing beside it - she presumed Thierry. Hannah got out and in English, but heavily accented, she asked him his name.

"Thierry Silber; where is Maddy?"

"Seeing to business; you have the bond?"

"Yes; you have the piece?"

"In the back."

"Once I've checked it, the payment can be made. I'm surprised Maddy isn't here herself."

Hannah ignored the comment and opened up the back of the van. Thierry looked inside and then made a call on a mobile phone. Hannah had never seen the like of it. Thierry stepped away from the rear of the van for privacy. A few minutes later, he returned.

"Okay; here's the bond," he said, handing an envelope to Hannah. She checked it and closed the rear door of the van. Pete got out and they walked away from the warehouse together, grabbing a cab as soon as possible for the rendezvous at the 80th Street apartment with Pierre who, having taken the call from Thierry, knew his masquerade as Michael was no longer required.

An hour later, they were all together and Hannah paid them.

"One hundred thousand dollars for you both, as agreed," she said as she handed over the cash.

"That's a lot of money, Maddy, for a short day's work," said Pierre, and Pete just nodded.

"Without you, it couldn't have worked, so it's well-earned ... and we were just lucky he was alone and there was no obvious danger. I do not like this style of handover; it's too risky."

"Someone is going to be very pissed very soon," suggested Pierre.

"And someone else is just about to wake up," announced Hannah.

She'd vacated the 23rd Street apartment, knowing that, within the hour, Michael would wake up and find himself locked in the trunk of the limousine - minus his dignity, though not his bronze. Hannah thought that was very gallant of her, seeing as he was plotting with Conan to end her promising career and Conan would, in the not-too-distant future, be mourning the loss of his half million dollars - but probably nursing his bruised ego more.

As for Thierry, he drove the security van to the airport and had the sculpture loaded onto a plane bound for Hong Kong, and then disappeared.

Hannah believed that Thierry was working on his own account. It seemed wrong that he would hand over the bond if the plan had originally been to clear her out. Maybe Michael and Conan were in on it together and Thierry saw a chance. When he had called Pierre at the time of the handover, he had simply asked if the piece had been moved and Pierre had confirmed that it had. So maybe they were in on it together and Michael needed the insurance, alleviating Conan of half a million dollars in the process. Where the fake sculpture was now, who knew?

Hannah sat quietly after the guys had gone and tallied up. The bond for five hundred and thirty thousand dollars was in her hand. The costs of the operation were covered by the three hundred thousand that she had received from the Californian for the auctioned *De Nizza*. The hundred and fifty thousand dollars profit on the original sale of that piece was bonus money, the emeralds having funded the hundred thousand she'd handed over at the benefit. The one hundred and fifty thousand she hadn't expected was deposited along with the bond.

The comment she had made to the guys weighed on her mind. The handover of a stolen masterpiece was fraught with danger and, had it not been for Pierre and Pete, she was certain that she wouldn't have been quite so lucky. A safer handover process was needed - and a cheaper one too! It had cost her one hundred thousand the last time and two hundred thousand this time. Of course, worth it to secure the payment but money that could have been invested elsewhere.

"Work alone, Hannah. Don't rely on anyone, trust no one and don't find yourself responsible for someone else; worrying about them distracts you from your purpose."

She didn't know whose voice it had been in her head. It wasn't her own; it sounded much older.

The following day, she went to see Luke and gave him his bonus, losing something of herself in the process but gaining some useful experience.

She packed and vacated the apartment and boarded a train for San Francisco.

This ability to melt away like ice gave her a special feeling, one of immense power and true freedom. She smiled for the first hour and then picked up her book - *Brave New World*, by Aldous Huxley.

Crime Five - Virtuoso

Chapter One – Steinway would be turning in his grave

Hannah found a small apartment behind Ghirardelli Square, a rear-facing unit with a small balcony, overlooking the Square and the water's edge beyond.

Up to this point, she had committed four crimes. In each case, she had used a number of disguises, and only now realised that she had a trademark or signature of sorts - the use of decoys, copies and fakes. She'd stolen the Degas, which was a fake, also leaving Hettie the fake Cartier lipstick case. She'd stolen both original and copy of the chalice and left a replica in its place in the display case. She'd masked Gerhardt's paintings with good quality prints to make him believe the security firm had delivered the wrong pictures to the yacht, giving her the opportunity to offer to take them back to the gallery and fetch the *correct* ones, instead, leaving him just a photograph of the painting she had teased him with. She'd led an associate to believe that he was exchanging half a million dollars for a magnificent bronze sculpture, which was, in fact, a clever copy made by a student friend.

Hannah had one million dollars in the bank, a very chic and stylish wardrobe, and a lot of valuable experience.

Shortly after she took up residence in the apartment, she had a piano delivered and advertised that she gave lessons. Within a week, it resulted in her obtaining two students, a girl and a shy boy - both aged thirteen: each belonging to very pushy and wealthy parents with homes in *The Heights*.

Perfect!

The choice of profession had been deliberate; wealthy, pushy parents always wanted their children to learn the piano. It made for frequent invitations to soirees and cultivated a perfectly simple and discrete image of the rather austere but incredibly talented pianist. Who would suspect her of harboring secrets and plans to steal their highly prized masterpieces? She liked to teach children the piano; they had less guarded tongues and let slip the most personal of details about their parents and their security systems!

Hannah's plan this time was to steal and then dispose of her ill-gotten gains rather than steal to order. She wanted to avoid the handover in draughty and deserted warehouses to heavyset men who probably carried guns. She didn't trust anyone, save Pierre and Pete, but she vowed that she would never use their services again. They were also beginning to learn too much about her; information that could be sold if the pension needed topping up. In her view, far better to trust no one; perhaps not going as far as mistrusting everyone; that didn't figure - teenage students with no real talent could be trusted.

The girl - Zoe - was pretty and tone deaf; the boy - Dominic - a little better and more conscientious. His parents made the first move and invited her to play for them at an evening with friends, celebrating the mother's fortieth birthday.

The big 4-0. That sounded scary as hell to Hannah; not yet twenty-four albeit acting twenty-eight this time. She was posing as *Valerie Bishop*, from Oxford; the accent was simple, and the city was one she knew well. Dominic gave her the invitation.

"Oh, thank you; crikey! The big 4-0 ... What does your mother like? I want to get her something."

"She collects thimbles," replied Dominic shyly.

"Does she; well, that's simple enough. Shall we practice a duet that we can play for her on her birthday?"

Dominic would have preferred to have sunk out of all trace than allow his parents to judge his performance. Hannah knew she could coach him and deliver a half-decent job.

Happy parents made for relaxed atmospheres, loose tongues and recommendations.

The party was two days hence, and all Hannah had to do was find a pretty, little thimble to provide the gift. Two antique shops later and the perfect Edwardian silver thimble was in the bag.

Hannah's goal was to inveigle herself in the upper echelons of the San Francisco society and steal something worth the bother; she practiced her half of the duet and a number of other pieces to clear her mind.

On the evening in question, dressed as *Laura Ashley* had intended a proper young woman from the Home Counties to look, she turned up at Dominic's house in *The Heights* and announced herself.

Chapter Two – Finding a thimble in a haystack

"It's Valerie, isn't it?" inquired the woman.

"Yes, that's right."

"I'm Dominic's mother, Francine; won't you come in? I'm so pleased you agreed to perform for us, and Dominic is very excited about the duet."

Hannah knew different. "He has a lot of potential."

"Does he?"

"Oh, I almost forgot; happy birthday!" said Hannah, handing over the gift and the card.

"Oh, really you shouldn't have; playing for us is enough."

"I hope you don't already have one like it," Hannah said as Francine opened the delicately wrapped box.

"Oh, my dear, this is perfect!"

"English, Edwardian silver..." added Hannah.

"I certainly don't have one like it as you will see ..."

They went into the main living room to meet the other guests; there were few because Hannah had arrived early, hoping that she and Dominic could practice a little before the performance. She met *the husband*, Charles, and sundry friends whose names she filed away carefully. Dominic was hiding, hoping to avoid the spotlight so she made a beeline, and they went to the music room to practice for half an hour.

"Don't worry; she'll love it. Just imagine you're at my place, and if we do really well then, I'll treat us next time you come over, okay?"

He didn't say much and just smiled in his pale, thin way. The poor lad was weighed down by all of the expectations and the not so gentle cajoling his parents dished out, believing they were instilling him with confidence. If they'd asked the lad what he wanted, they would have heard something about computers and software, but it all got lost in the arguments.

Francine appeared.

"Time to get ready; nearly everyone is here," she announced.

Hannah grabbed Dominic's hand and held it as they walked into the main room where the grand piano was set up. Francine introduced Hannah as "Valerie", and she and Dominic took up their places.

They played their little piece and Dominic, presumably trying to please Hannah as much as his mother, did a reasonable job and only faltered once, which Hannah expertly covered up. The applause was good natured, and once the ordeal was over, Dominic relaxed and was allowed to escape. Francine waltzed over to Hannah and handed her a glass of champagne.

"Thank you, Valerie; that was lovely."

"I have some other pieces to play for you when you want," Hannah offered.

"Great! I have something to show you; you weren't the only one who gave me a thimble ..."

Francine towed her to a table upon which the gifts were piled; she noticed that hers was already buried.

"Look! It's glass, and has the most exquisite little rose encased in it; apparently it was once owned by Marie-Antoinette ..."

Hannah cooed as required, and immediately felt the two pairs of eyes of the givers; they were milking it for everything it had to offer.

"It's beautiful!" exclaimed Hannah.

Francine was called away. Hannah scanned the room for the couple. She found a mature pair of hawkish social grandees; older by ten years than the average guest; clearly solid wealth - apparently built on shipping she later discovered - and residents of *The Broadway*.

"Bingo!" said Hannah to herself as she inched in their direction, hoping to get introduced.

"Valerie!" It was Francine. "Let me introduce you to Loretta and David Colton."

"Hello," Hannah offered a little shyly.

"My dear, you play beautifully; I did too in my youth. Let's spice this up with a duet of our own, shall we?"

Loretta Colton needed no encouragement to display her talents; David just looked on proudly.

"*Ragtime*; that'll get the heels tapping," she suggested.

She and Hannah banged it out, and it was evident that the woman could play; the applause was suitably appreciative.

"I have a party in a week; please come and play for us," she said to Hannah.

"I'd be delighted but only if you promise to play another duet."

Loretta tittered, and then got waylaid by several of the other women, leaving Hannah alone momentarily. David appeared at her elbow.

"Excuse Loretta; she is very *energetic* at times."

Hannah turned to address him.

"Oh, not at all; she does play very well."

"She had a very promising career ahead of her but gave it all up to be my wife."

"How long have you been married?" Hannah asked politely.

"Twenty-five years this year - sadly no children," he added wistfully, and Hannah assumed the "fault" lay with Loretta.

"Gosh; that's nearly as old as me!" Hannah exclaimed.

"Are you planning to stay in the city long?" David asked, and Hannah recognized the tone - all *frisky goat* albeit tempered.

"A couple of months, maybe longer; depends on work."

"You teach the piano?"

"Yes, and I translate legal documents into French, Spanish and German."

"My! Such hidden talents. I may have some work for you in that line; I'll speak to you more at the party next week."

"Okay; that'll be super," said Hannah, smiling sweetly; then becoming aware of Loretta's diamond-cut, laser-guided pupils on her back, she realized that she knew the *score* of this tune all too well.

The party proceeded as most do. Hannah played again and played "Happy Birthday" as the cake with the forty candles was brought out. Francine blew them all out in three goes and after that, things drifted and people started to leave. Hannah wasn't sure when she should make her escape. At that precise second, Francine cornered her.

"Let me show you the collection," she said with an undertone that Hannah translated as 'we need to talk'.

They ascended two flights of stairs and found themselves on a broad landing, which was lined with display cases. Each case was literally stuffed with thimbles.

"It has taken years and years," said Francine, and Hannah was impressed for there were hundreds.

"Why thimbles?" Hannah asked.

"Oh; I don't know. They're perfect, aren't they? So decorative and so useful ... David has a reputation ..."

There it was.

"He says he might have some work for me."

"Yes ... just be careful to keep the relationship on a strictly business footing, for Loretta's sake *and* your own; he is not, how shall we say it, considerate of the young woman's feelings."

"Or Loretta's for that matter," added Hannah, hoping to signal she wasn't as green as she was cabbage looking.

"Quite ... I think I'll put yours here," she said, pointing to a space in the third cabinet.

"And Loretta's?" asked Hannah.

"Oh; here," Francine replied, pointing to a completely empty shelf, "it's been waiting for a very long time."

They descended, and Loretta caught a glance as they did and there was a kind of nod between her and Francine. To Hannah, the cost of the gift - David had deliberately slipped that it was fifty thousand dollars - suddenly seemed like a small price to pay for someone like Francine to watch your back.

"I'll be off then," announced Hannah, "thank you so much for inviting me."

"Not at all, and Dominic so looks forward to his lessons. We'll see you at Loretta's next week by all accounts."

Hannah paid her respects to Loretta and David and left with the invitation tucked in her purse ... and a whole load to think about!

Chapter Three – Loretta's bash

Hannah practiced really hard for the party, and researched the Colton's as deeply as she could, even spying on the house in *The Broadway*, which was magnificent.

The Colton's were not collectors, not of art anyway, not seriously, but nevertheless patrons, and always at the top of the donations lists. It was Loretta's money and not David's. She had inherited the shipping money and, as a lonely, barren heiress, had looked for adventure and had found David. He was dangerously handsome, confident, stylish and as poor as a church mouse. They had married without a prenuptial agreement, so Hannah was pretty sure that Loretta forgave all sorts of indiscretions just to keep out of the divorce court and avoid the risk of losing any of her three hundred millions. David had worked and still worked for one of the companies but in a role where he could do the least amount of damage and earn the highest salary to fund his excesses, which Loretta neither wished to know about or meet in the street.

Hannah wondered if they had anything of real importance to steal at all. She couldn't wait for the party and the chance to have a nose about. It came round quickly enough and suddenly she was ringing at their bell. A butler-style person answered and showed her in. She was immediately nabbed by Loretta.

"Valerie! So pleased you were able to come; I hope you've been practicing."

"Oh yes; very hard. I didn't want to let you down."

"Sweet child." and with that Hannah was fairly well catapulted into the fray and within fifteen minutes was dueting with Loretta, who seemed a trifle high - a self-medicating manic depressive was Hannah's conclusion and overdoing the *uppers* this evening. She was released after twenty minutes to get a drink and mingle. She sought out Francine and Charles to say hello, who showed less than the expected enthusiasm. Brushed off, she found David.

"Ah! Valerie; good to see you. Remember I said that I might I have some work for you; I do. Drop by the office on Tuesday at eleven and I'll run it by you." He handed her his business card.

"Thank you! That is extraordinarily kind," she returned, feeling the tell-tale stabs in her back, which she ignored, seeing as she had been brushed off for no apparent reason ... or perhaps the *work* had already been discussed and it heralded potential trouble.

Hannah mingled, wishing she knew a reliable man so that she could have brought a partner. Scanning everywhere open to view, she saw nothing except modern and tasteless art that was worthless; her mind wandered back to Francine's thimble, as a potential consolation prize.

"Valerie!"

It was Loretta.

"Come with me; I simply must show you something ..."

Those magic words that Hannah recognized in seven languages. She was towed to one of the upper floors.

"I simply have to show you this; it's a wreck at the moment but after restoration it will be so pretty ..."

In a room off the corridor was a harpsichord, a very old harpsichord that was in dire need of restoration, but the instrument was unequalled in its provenance.

"One of perhaps only two or three that are accredited to *Zenti*, made in 1666. This one is called the *Nightingale*. Sit; play!" urged Loretta, and Hannah sat and practiced her scales before picking out *Clair du Lune*.

"Exquisite!" Loretta added ecstatically.

"Who is doing the restoration?" Hannah asked.

"Fitzwilliam's; the finest in the country. I would send it back to Italy but that seems unpatriotic ... as if it wasn't costing enough already."

"Fitzwilliam's has a world class reputation," added Hannah, not wishing to see the piece disappear to Europe anytime soon!

"When it is restored, we will host a gala evening and raise money for *Feeding America*."

"How long will it take?"

"Three months at least."

"Oh; I may have returned to England by then; it depends on this work of David's and how the teaching goes."

"Let's hope both keep you here until after the gala." But Hannah was pretty sure that Loretta didn't actually give a damn if they did. "When are you meeting David?"

"Tuesday."

"Meet me for lunch afterwards, won't you?"

"Oh, really? That would be lovely ..."

They descended, and Hannah knew the lunch invitation was deliberate so that David couldn't monopolize her or whatever it was that he was planning to do.

Hannah was again abandoned, and she toyed with disappearing but it had only been an hour so that felt rude although she had played. She played again, by herself; something familiar and not too loud, just to keep herself from getting bored and, after half an hour, she decided it was time to go. She sought out her hosts to thank them and to say goodbye; they were in the hall bidding farewell to someone else.

"Thank you for inviting me and for showing me the harpsichord," Hannah said very politely.

"Not at all, Valerie, and we'll see you on Tuesday. David promises to be through with you by twelve-thirty so that we can have lunch."

David said nothing and just smiled. Hannah knew that smile, the "fifteen-all" smile of combatant couples.

"Goodbye!" she said, and left, choosing to walk the relatively short distance back to the apartment which cleared her head. A plan began to emerge.

"A world class if not a world-renowned harpsichord ..." Hannah mused.

Unlike Stradivarius' violins, which perhaps most people would have heard of, most would probably not have heard of *Zenti* and his fabled instrument the *Nightingale*. Hannah had but then she knew a good deal more about most things than most people. "A cunning switch, after the restoration; no point stealing a wreck and incurring the costs of doing it up; I need a similar instrument ... and a date with Fitzwilliam's!"

On the Monday, she found a battered old harpsichord that was roughly the same shape as Loretta's. It was allegedly very old, perhaps Flemish and even from the studio of *Couchet*, but this was unimportant. She called Fitzwilliam's and discussed the project.

"We would be delighted to undertake the project, Frau Bohm; of course, we shall need to see it before we can estimate how long the work will take or indeed, how much it will cost."

"Naturally, Jonas; I would like it painted in the style of the *Nightingale*..." Hannah was already on the inside track. "I'll have it delivered to you and then come in to discuss the restoration *but* it simply has to be ready in two months."

"I'm sure we can accommodate that," Jonas assured her, and Hannah was pretty sure that for a price, they could accommodate anything.

The party at Loretta's hadn't been a waste of time at all and this work for David could be interesting. Regular contact with the Colton's would be essential if the switch was going to be effected - again a decoy and again timing had to be perfect; not only that, but her disguise as Loretta Colton would also need to be flawless!

Chapter Four – David's offer of work and lunch

Hannah dressed very smartly although plainly, and headed to David's office in Battery Street for the appointment at eleven o'clock on the Tuesday. She announced herself, and within five minutes, his secretary came to collect her from reception. The woman was older and in the "battle axe" category, so Hannah guessed that Loretta must have had a hand in her selection.

"Please wait here, Ms. Bishop, and Mr. Colton will see you shortly," she said and parked Hannah in another reception-style area and disappeared behind some frosted glass. Five minutes later, David appeared.

"Valerie! So good to see you; come in, won't you?"

She entered his office, which looked like a play den, and he instantly offered her a drink.

"Just tea, please," she said, refusing the scotch.

The order for tea was placed and David motioned to Hannah to sit down at the small conference table which afforded views of Telegraph Hill.

"Was it translation work you had in mind, David?" Hannah asked, seizing the initiative.

"Yes, it was. I have a contract dispute with a business in Europe and the damn lawyers are taking an age to translate the original contracts; I was hoping you could do the job ..."

"What language are the contracts written in?"

"German; this was twenty years ago. Everything was fine until some problem arose and then they started referring back to these damn papers which no one could find or read when they did. I'm sure it's a ploy to avoid some costs that will fall to them."

"I'll do my best; it would help if you could tell me what the contract is for."

"Various consultancy and advisory services over a number of engineering projects."

"Basically, a tax swindle then?" Hannah said with pluck, and David erupted with laughter.

"Creative accounting, yes," he managed eventually.

"If you can let me have a copy, I'll get started straight away. When do you want them by?"

"Two weeks?"

"That should be fine. I have no idea how much to charge you," Hannah offered innocently.

"There are two contracts; let's say a thousand dollars each, shall we?"

"Okay ... Why haven't you employed a translator before now?"

"Well, here's the thing; it was in our favour to let this drag until now but the game has changed and now, we need to be absolutely sure about what the contracts say and where the liability falls; if it falls to us then the costs are ghastly and-"

"Your arse will be on the line ..."

"I might even have to resign."

"Then the sooner I start, the better."

"I'd rather you didn't speak to Loretta about this in detail; as far as she is concerned, it's a simple translation job. I don't want to upset her." David's look suggested it might just be the straw that broke the camel's back, and divorce would be next.

"You can rely on my absolute discretion, David," Hannah stated solidly.

"I knew I could," he replied as he handed over an envelope that contained the contracts.

"Let's meet in a week and discuss progress, shall we?"

"Okay; I'll aim to have one ready by then."

"Good. So, lunch with Loretta now; excellent!"

Without forewarning or ceremony, Loretta walked in.

"Loretta!" exclaimed David like the dutiful husband.

"Hello, Loretta," said Hannah, smiling.

"Business done? Shall we, Valerie?"

"Yes," Hannah replied, and watched as Loretta planted a cold little kiss on David's cheek. As Hannah turned to leave, she bid David farewell, "See you soon, David."

"Goodbye, Valerie; any problems just call."

The women left, and it was only after they had vacated the building that Loretta actually spoke.

"I've invited Francine to join us; I hope you don't mind," she said as they headed to the car waiting at the curbside.

"Not at all ..." said Hannah, and she ticked off another correct prediction.

The car took them to a smart little Italian restaurant on Lombard Street where Francine was waiting.

"Valerie!" she said with an almost maternal smile on her lips.

"Francine; so nice to see you."

"How did it go with David?"

"Fine," she replied bluntly but politely and as a way of diverting attention she added, "I wondered if Dominic would be willing to play at the gala, which Loretta has suggested would be the perfect way to unveil the harpsichord after its restoration."

"I'm sure he'd be thrilled, especially if you tutor him; he likes you very much."

"He's a sweet boy ..."

"It's a lovely idea, Valerie; the young man needs to build his confidence and extend his repertoire," said Loretta.

Lunch proceeded, and Hannah used the opportunity to study Loretta very closely.

"When is the *Nightingale* being moved to Fitzwilliam's, Loretta?"

"On Thursday; three months they say for sure, now that someone else has delivered a harpsichord for restoration. I said to Jonas, 'I was first, and the *Nightingale* is an important instrument'..."

"I'm sure they won't let you down, Loretta, especially if they know the gala is planned," said Hannah

"They had better not!" Loretta replied hotly.

Lunch for Hannah was a tasteless affair; the other two women were mindful of her for the sake of appearances and nothing confidential was discussed, just mindless tittle-tattle, and Hannah excused herself before they had all finished, citing that she needed to get ready for a lesson.

"See you soon," they cooed, and Hannah suddenly found herself outside of the inner wheel. She cared little because she wanted to read the contracts and find out just how far up to his neck David was *and* how that might profit her in the end.

Chapter Five – The contracts and the appointment at Fitzwilliam's

In the quiet solitude of the apartment, she read the contracts and dictated the translation for typing up later. After three hours, she had them translated and, more importantly, dissected.

David had been engaged by a company in Germany to provide consultancy and advisory services to them over a number of large engineering projects - the contract had been running for a very long time and was very profitable. Then there were some problems and the basis of the dispute, as far as she could determine from the few letters that were in the envelope with the copy of the contracts, was that they held David responsible for some failings and they were suing him for malpractice or negligence. In order to get her two thousand dollars, she dictated the translation of the contracts and then started to investigate the company that was suing David. She surmised that he probably hadn't done what they had paid him to do; and he was hoping for a get out clause in the contract rather than face the showdown.

Nothing on the face of it suggested that there was any profit in the contracts or the dispute for Hannah herself except the option to tell Loretta before David did or blackmail him to keep her mouth shut for the time being.

The translation and the cogitation had taken up the rest of the day and most of the evening, so she retired because the following day she had the appointment at Fitzwilliam's to discuss the restoration of her harpsichord just ahead of Loretta's own appointment on the Thursday.

Her disguise was that of an Austrian woman, of about forty, called *Frau Anna Bohm* - a professional musician and music teacher. The harpsichord she had bought for two hundred dollars minus its innards had already been delivered to the workshop on Jones Street in Lower Nob Hill.

oOo

"Frau Bohm; I am delighted to make your acquaintance and thank you for putting your trust in our work; it's an interesting piece though sadly not a *Zenti*."

"It is of no consequence, Jonas; it is really only the case that I want restored and painted. I like the idea of using it to house a modern mechanism even an electronic keyboard; let's leave that decision until you've had a good look."

"Why painted like the *Nightingale*?"

"It's an instrument we all know, and a little bird tells me that your workshop has the job of restoring it for Loretta Colton."

Hannah deliberately went for broke.

"It is not something I can discuss but if you were to drop by in, say, a few days, you might have a pleasant surprise," suggested Jonas.

They shared a conspiratorial smile, and Hannah left to give Dominic his lesson.

"Dominic ... What do you really want to do?"

"Build computers."

"Really! I like them too. How about as a treat, and I said we would have a treat after your mother's birthday party performance, we build one together? Not a computer exactly; more like a synthesizer."

"Why a synthesizer?"

"I teach music and often it's helpful to hear different sounds ... Do you think you could help me?"

"Absolutely!" and for the first time, she saw the real Dominic.

"We shan't say anything to your parents, *and* you will still have to play the piano too. As a surprise, we'll compose a piece of music that we can play for them on the synthesizer, and when they see your handiwork, you might just get their permission to build your computer."

"That would be really, really, cool!"

"Excellent!"

Hannah was hatching a plan and it resembled a ball of string; knotted and twisted, the end lost in the swirling mass of fibres. Hannah could see a pretty little harpsichord being unveiled at a gala event, capturing everyone's attention, drawing the eye away from the obvious flaw, which was that the beautifully restored *Nightingale* had a plug and was connected to a wall socket!

Dominic left and Hannah headed into town to find the components for the synthesizer.

Chapter Six – Friday and Hannah sneaks a peek

On Friday, as Frau Bohm, Hannah revisited the workshop to get a peek at the *Nightingale*, which had been delivered the day before.

"Frau Bohm; can you follow me?" said Jonas and he escorted her to a private area of the workshop and threw back the cover that was hiding the *Nightingale*.

"It's *so* beautiful!" she trilled, "Loretta Colton is extremely lucky."

"She is one of the few people who really appreciates its quality *and* she is willing to invest in it for the future ..."

"Now that I see it, I am convinced that mine should be painted exactly like it, as a kind of homage."

"If you're sure because the restorer will do both at the same time if that is the case."

"It should be the same; if I can't have the original then at least a copy by the same restorer."

"It is agreed, and two months will be no problem as it is just the casing. The *Nightingale* will take three and I'm informed it will be unveiled at a special gala evening where Loretta will play and, apparently, Dominic Belden."

"The Belden boy, yes, his parents approached me, but I referred them to a colleague, Valerie Bishop; she is younger and has more patience with children."

"Stop by anytime, Frau Bohm; but avoid the workshop for the next month."

"Why?"

"In my experience, most owners simply break down when they see their instrument laying in pieces; it's part of the process but much like open heart surgery before the chest is sewed back up."

"I'm fascinated by surgery but I take your point."

Hannah left and went home to compose the piece of music that she wanted Dominic to play on the evening of the gala.

She typed up the translation of the contracts and intended to deliver both to David on the following Tuesday and get her two thousand dollars. That would pay for the synthesizer and a transport case for the instrument. She knew that once the *Nightingale* was delivered to the gala venue, Loretta would not be able to stay away and would insist on seeing her prized possession. Therefore, the switch would need to occur after that, and she would need to get her instrument in and Loretta's out undetected. Her intended cover was that of a tuner; a skill she was practicing very hard.

One thing remained to do; decide whether to blackmail David or actually help him. She couldn't decide; not that there was much she could do. "If he's signed off fake engineer's reports for his fee and the German company has found him out then he's basically screwed."

In the end, she decided just to deliver the translations and then perhaps tell Loretta on the evening of the gala by way of a distraction. It was partly Loretta's fault anyway thought Hannah, she'd spoilt him out of guilt for not being able to deliver a child and he'd taken full advantage of it.

Hannah spent the weekend studying modern electronics and synthesizers, ending the weekend by debuting her first original composition on the hired piano.

Chapter Seven – David and Dominic

David must have had a threat because although he was charm itself on the Tuesday when Hannah delivered the translations, he was careful to have the secretary in full view the entire time and she never budged from her seat. He paid over the two thousand dollars in cash and thanked her but with less than his usual *joie de vivre*.

Dominic was much more enthusiastic when he arrived, especially as Hannah had everything laid out for him to see. But before he could touch any of it, she made him play her composition, which he loved and sailed through. Together they worked on the synthesizer and, within two weeks, had it nearly working. They were just about ready to play her piece on it when Hannah asked a question.

"Does your mother clean all of those thimbles herself? It must take an age."

"Oh yes; Gillian isn't allowed to go near the cases; she doesn't even have a key - mom keeps that in the jewellery box on her dresser. Once a month, she takes them all out and cleans them; it takes all day!"

"Did she say you could definitely play at the gala?"

"Yes ..." spoken less energetically, "Loretta wants me to practice a duet with her to play on the harpsichord. You'll be there though, right?"

"Oh yes; don't worry; I'll be there ..."

"We're nearly done."

"Yep; next lesson we'll have it working and then I want to practise the new piece on it ... Try not to worry about the gala; when you're a little older, you'll appreciate what you've learned and achieved, so much more than you do now."

He left happy and Hannah just had time to pop into Jonas's workshop to assess progress and check some vital measurements.

"I'd like the legs to be collapsible and for it all to be able to fit into a transport trolley; I'll have that delivered next week, Jonas."

"No problem; do you want to see them?"

"Can I?"

He let her into the private space and both instruments looked like, well, bleached skeletons; all the rot and decay, dirt and grime had been removed and the surfaces were being prepared for the painting.

"We have preserved as much of the original painting on the *Nightingale* as was possible, but it was in very poor condition. Yours was in an even less good state but as you can see, there is some carving which is now revealed, and the hinges of the lid are definitely Flemish and of the time so our belief that it could be a *Couchet* is probably right."

"Excellent! I'd like to take some measurements so that the keyboard can be made to fit perfectly, could you help me?"

They took all the measurements that Hannah needed to ensure that the keyboard fitted snuggly, especially for travelling; after which she left, minus an "on account payment" of five thousand dollars, being half the eventual cost of the restoration. Still, the *Zenti*, fully restored, would fetch one hundred thousand or even one hundred and fifty, and finding a buyer was her next task.

Chapter Eight – Fencing lessons

She mused that good old Rathbone would probably have known where to offload the piece; and taking the *Nightingale* out of the country, possibly back to Europe, was a very real consideration. It was the one drawback of not stealing to order; you were lumbered with the piece until you could get shot of it but that was preferable to being shot at!

She scoured the newspapers at the library for the names of all the men convicted of handling stolen property, and made a list of those who, on the basis of their original sentencing, should be out and about. Some still lived in San Francisco according to the phone book. Finding ex-felons was relatively easy; asking them if they were still in their original line of business, somewhat trickier.

Two appeared to be running businesses, one an antique shop, which seemed a little too obvious and the other had a dry-cleaning place just off the square, a stone's throw from the apartment. She spilt some red wine over a silk scarf and took it in, hoping to see *Bob Andrews* in person.

"That shouldn't be too much of a problem ... but I'll need to ask you to pay in advance," he said.

"Oh, sure," replied Hannah as *Sadie Goldberg*, and she ferreted in her purse only to *accidentally* tumble out a rather pretty cameo brooch.

"Is it Italian?" he asked with more than an ounce of curiosity.

"My grandmother's *and* she was Italian, so probably. It's causing me sleepless nights."

"How so?"

"There was a break-in and everything of value was stolen - or so I thought. I reported it and claimed on the insurance and then I found this and now I feel like a criminal because I had the insurance money and I should really give it to them but then they might think I hid it and other things ... I really just want shot of it; I can't sell it in case it turns up and someone remembers it was mine."

Hannah screwed out a few tears.

"Don't cry; if you really did want to get rid of it then I could take it off your hands. I can't give you much for it, but you'd never see it again and no one would be the wiser."

Hannah looked him squarely in the face and smiled through the tears and said, "You would do that for me?"

"Of course; I used to deal in antiques; I have connections. How much did you get back from the insurance company for it?"

"Seven hundred and fifty dollars."

"What say I give you two hundred and fifty and you never have to see it again?"

"Thank you so much!" and Hannah opened the floodgates and allowed him to put his arm around her shoulder as he gave her his handkerchief.

"There, there; it's all over."

She wiped her eyes, and he gave her the money. She left, thanking him profusely.

"Still in business; let's put a big fat worm on this hook, shall we?" she said to herself as she donned the disguise of Anna Bohm, wending her way back to the Square, where she waited for Bob Andrews to leave so she could follow him.

At five o'clock, he closed up and she downed the dregs of her coffee and watched for his likely route; she hoped he didn't just jump in a car. He didn't and he walked and ended up at the antique shop of the other man who had been convicted for handling stolen goods - now partners in crime after their time spent together in the penitentiary. Hannah walked in; they were both in the back and she idled through the stuff on display and inched nearer to the counter so that she could overhear their conversation.

"Be with you in a minute!" the other man called out.

Hannah said nothing and walked around, eyeing a few things that might be worth buying and selling on. The man appeared.

"Hi! Sorry; did you need any help? Looking for something specific?" he asked.

"No, not really; maybe the hand painted fan ... Is it Chinese?"

"Yes," he said, and she knew from his face that he was getting his facts ready before launching into his pitch.

She toyed with it and then spied some sheet music.

"There are some very old pieces in the box, but to be honest, no one much cares for it these days; I'll let you have the lot for fifty dollars ..."

Hannah turned and smiled and then rifled through the box to see if there was anything interesting; job lots had a remarkable habit of throwing up the most unexpected surprises.

"I'll take the lot for thirty-five ..."

"Forty ..."

"Deal!"

"Do you play?" he asked

"Yes; the piano. I'm actually looking to sell an instrument; a rare Eighteenth Century Italian harpsichord; it has an uncertain provenance ..."

Hannah adopted a tone, a tell-tale inflection.

"I only know of one in the city," he said with a wicked glint in his eye.

"Then are you interested?"

"For the right price."

"One hundred and fifty thousand dollars, fully restored by Fitzwilliam's."

"When could I take possession?"

"In about three months ..."

"That would give me time to line up a buyer, so that would work ..."

Hannah smiled and put the sheet music on the counter with two twenty-dollar bills.

"I'll be in touch."

"Fine ..."

She quit the shop and headed straight to the apartment only then allowing herself to breathe.

"Did I just do what I think I just did?" she asked herself, and her hands were still shaking.

Chapter Nine – The plan takes shape

Hannah got the travel trolley made for the harpsichord and had it delivered to the workshop, calling in briefly to assess progress, finding the artist-restorer was painting the casings.

"It's painstaking work," injected Jonas.

"But worth it in the end," she replied.

Next up was completing the piece for the gala, and when Dominic came in, she got him to play it on the synthesizer. It made a pretty authentic sound but was still unmistakably manufactured.

"How can we make this sound better?"

"Well, once the synthesizer is housed in a casing then that will probably help."

"I think you're right. If it was wooden then the sound would be softer; perhaps we need better speakers too. They twiddled and faddled and all the while, Hannah was aiming her questions closer and closer to the target.

"Are you going somewhere nice for the holidays?" she asked.

"Mr. and Mrs. Colton want us all to go to Mexico."

"Wow; how exciting!"

"Yeah ..." spoken with even less than the usual enthusiasm

"Where would you like to go?"

"I want to go to see the launch of *Columbia*."

"I'd love to see that too; perhaps we could go together ... When is it?"

"Two days after the gala."

"That is cutting it a bit fine; perhaps I should talk to your parents. If some of your friends wanted to go and there were enough adults to supervise, I'm sure they'd be happy. When were Mr. and Mrs. Colton planning to go to Mexico?"

"About the same time."

"You could go to the rocket launch and then fly on to Mexico ... How about I come over one day soon so that you can play the gala piece for your parents, and I'll talk to them then?"

"*Please*," implored the lad.

"It would be very exciting, wouldn't it?"

They twiddled and faddled some more with the keyboard; Dominic left in high spirits.

"They're out of the country and I have the perfect alibi ... timing would have to be perfect ... but that thimble will be mine ... and what wouldn't I give to see her face when she realizes it's missing!"

The following day, Hannah got up and decided she would be Loretta Colton for the day. Her disguise as the fifty-year-old socialite was coming on but making herself look fifty was very hard; thankfully, Loretta was not showing too many signs of her age. Her deportment was the key *and* the frequent shifts between mania and depression. The acid test, a visit to David at the office, a fleeting visit to set the cat amongst the pigeons over the contract debacle. If she could fool David, just for a few minutes, then surely everyone else would believe it and Hannah knew that if you expected to see a person then you often did "see" the person and minor things got overlooked. Maybe that wouldn't be true in the case of Francine; she seemed to be the sort to scrutinize, evidently looking for the flaws that made her feel so much better about herself.

Hannah dressed and applied her make-up, practising the little speech that she intended to deliver. She donned a headscarf and dark glasses. She'd found decent lookalike rings and, thankfully, the woman seemed only to wear a simple single strand of pearls most of the time.

"Here goes!"

At the office, Hannah merely strode in and waved her hand at security in that terribly dismissive fashion of Loretta's in response to the expected greeting - well, she did own the building! Hannah took the elevator and exited into the outer reception area and strode confidently to the office door to find David sat as his desk with the receptionist at his side, standing a little too close.

"Loretta!"

"David; I just wanted to tell you that I forgive you unconditionally over the discrepancies with the German contract; go and tell Douglas everything and I'll pay the penalties ..."

"You will?"

"Of course, darling; we can't have this hanging over our heads - must run, see you later!"

Hannah turned and strode out, taking the stairs so that she didn't have to wait for the elevator and risk getting waylaid.

Oh to be a fly on the wall!

Hannah marched through reception and out into the street, grabbing a cab as soon as possible, giving the address of the antique shop where she'd bought the music. Hannah assumed that the shop owner would know of Loretta but would probably not have seen her up close.

The cab dropped her off.

"Good morning, Mrs. Colton!" said the owner, "Was the gift well received?"

"Shit!" said Hannah to herself but kept calm.

"Francine absolutely loved it; I'm looking for something similar ..."

"I have another glass thimble but not quite in that league, probably a copy. It's Eighteenth Century, but as you will see, the rose is painted onto the surface and not encased in the glass itself."

"Please show me!" Hannah demanded with the all too familiar mania.

He fetched it and placed it in her gloved palm.

"I'll take it!"

"I'll box it and get the receipt written out, cash or card, Mrs. Colton?"

"Cash ..."

Hannah handed over the thirteen hundred dollars and within a couple of minutes, had the thimble and a receipt bearing Loretta's name and address.

"Thank you *so* much!"

"A little bird tells me you have a new playing partner ..."

Hannah assumed he meant the harpsichord.

"Hush; no one must know until the unveiling at the gala," she whispered.

"Right you are; is it the *Nightingale*?"

Hannah just smiled and left.

Dressed as Valerie, she went to see Francine on the pretence of giving Dominic the music to practice and to see how far the pigeons had flown.

"Valerie! What a lovely surprise," exclaimed Francine, "Come in ..."

"Thank you; I've finalized the piece for the gala and I wanted Dominic to have it to practise ..."

She handed over the score.

"Dominic has told us about your idea to get a group together to go to the launch of the Space Shuttle ..."

"I know he's very keen to go, and it would seem to make for the perfect start to the holidays; do you think it would work?"

"He's asking around to his friends to see who else is interested, and I said to Charles that it would be a splendid way of rewarding him for his hard work over the gala thing."

"Excellent! After the launch, we can get him on the flight to Mexico, and I'll be well-placed to get my flight back to the UK."

"You're heading back?"

"Yes; my mother is going into hospital and my father asked me to return so that I can be there to help when she comes out."

"Nothing serious I hope."

"Hysterectomy."

"Ah ..."

"May I see the thimble now that it's in its rightful place?" asked Hannah.

"Of course, my dear ..."

She was escorted back up to the landing where the cabinets were housed, and Francine made a beeline for the case where the glass thimble now sat on a black velvet cushion, occupying a shelf all by itself.

"Just beautiful," cooed Hannah.

"Loretta was very generous this year; I guess because it was my fortieth. The trip to Mexico was her idea too; we're all fascinated by the Mayan temples, and Charles has promised me a week on the beach after the "archaeological" bit ..."

"When do you leave exactly?"

"The morning of the second day after the gala ..."

"That is the day of the launch and I think the launch is in the afternoon. I could get Dominic on the next available flight on the morning afterwards so he'll only be one day later than you."

"It'll work out perfectly ... Did you do the translation work for David?"

"Oh yes - within the first week; it was pretty straightforward. I did them quickly because he said there were some questions that needed to be answered; not that he was specific but it sounded urgent ..."

"Quite so ... Would you like some tea, or do you have to run?"

"Unfortunately, I have to run; I'll see you soon."

Hannah left and interpreted the question over the contracts as a sign that Francine knew something but nothing specific; it was probably too early for David to have returned home and for he and Loretta to have had their conversation. Hannah was sure that once they had, the whole of the neighborhood would know that there was a problem with the contracts!

Chapter Ten – Revelations

It happened like this; David went to see the company lawyer - Douglas - and told him everything.

"And Loretta will pay the penalties?"

"That's what she said earlier; I'm on my way home now to give her a full report."

"The penalties amount to a staggering ten million dollars."

"Yes; I know ..."

Feeling a little ashamed of himself but better for having told Douglas everything, he went home fully expecting to have the perfect evening with Loretta who had been quite cold of late.

In the meantime, Douglas phoned Loretta and gave her the news about the penalties.

"Douglas; I don't have a clue what you're talking about; I haven't been to the office today."

Douglas recounted the whole episode. She was left stunned, and remained immobilized until David walked in.

"Loretta; what's wrong?" he asked, genuinely concerned.

"Douglas just called and told me the strangest thing; I have no recollection of visiting the office today, yet I did; neither do I recall knowing anything about the problems with the German contracts but apparently I know everything and have sworn to pay the penalties of ten million dollars."

"You were there; at the door to the office and after you told me that you knew about the problems and would pay the costs, you left very quickly. I didn't have time to catch you before you'd disappeared; did you take your pills?"

"I'm sure I did; but if this is all true then how did I find out about the problems with the contracts because for certain YOU DIDN'T TELL ME!"

"Loretta, please; calm down!"

She didn't calm down and, in the end, she threw him out.

"I'LL PAY THOSE COSTS, DAVID; IT'LL BE YOUR DIVORCE SETTLEMENT. YOU'LL NOT GET ONE CENT MORE FROM ME!"

He went to see Charles but this was after Hannah had called on Francine. He spoke confidentially to Charles, who of course, told Francine, who went straight round to see Loretta, who was gaily ripping her husband's wardrobe to shreds.

This was exactly the kind of distraction that Hannah was hoping for; not that she found out for some days, and it was only when Dominic said that the Colton's weren't now going to Mexico.

"Oh, what a pity! What happened to make them change their minds?"

"They're getting a divorce; I heard mom say so to dad."

"Really? How dreadfully upsetting ..."

"But we're still going, and I can definitely go to the launch if you'll come with me and make sure I get the plane the next day to Mexico."

"Of course; we'll make all the arrangements the next time I see your parents."

"Did you get the new speakers and see about the casing?"

"I did!"

By the time he left, the sound of the instrument was getting pretty close to what Hannah wanted but the final adjustments would have to wait until the casing was ready and that was still another whole month away.

That evening she spent a good part of it filing the key blank she had purchased so that it matched up to the impression of Dominic's door key that she had taken whilst he'd had his head in the electronic guts of the synthesizer. Happy with her progress on that front, she started to go through the sheet music she had bought at the antique shop.

"Oh, Hannah!"

Chapter Eleven – Ten thousand dollars later

Ten thousand dollars was going to be the eventual cost of the restoration but for that Hannah was getting a faithful copy of the *Nightingale*. The two thousand dollars that David had given her had paid for the synthesizer and the travel trolley.

"So far so good ..." was her own assessment.

She and Dominic debuted the piece on the synthesizer, which she took over to his house in a make-shift casing, and his parents were delighted. So much so that the objections over his own project of building a computer were fairly well quashed.

"You have a way with children, Valerie," said Francine, "Are you planning to have a family of your own?"

"Someday; when I meet the right one."

"Loretta is feeling unwell, and it looks likely that she and David will not be joining us in Mexico."

"But that's not for another two months; won't she have recovered by then?"

Francine said nothing and just gave her that look that said "it is going to take a very long time ..."

"I'll pop in and see her," ventured Hannah.

"Yes; do that ..."

Hannah did and found the spent shell that was once Loretta.

"Oh, Valerie ... how nice of you to call," she managed.

"Francine said you were feeling unwell, and I wondered if there was anything I could do for you."

"Such a thoughtful girl; perhaps I could ask you to play at the gala - my duet with Dominic; I feel sure that I won't be up to it."

"Of course; but that's still two months away, Loretta; I'm sure you'll have recovered your strength by then ... Where's David?"

Hannah got it all through the agonized and bitter sobs.

"What will people say when they find out?"

"No one need know, Loretta; Charles and Francine won't say anything and I'm sure I won't ..."

"Everyone has expected it for years, but you know, I really thought that as we got older, we'd work it all out."

"Perhaps you just need a break; to shed new light on things. Do you think you can forgive him?"

"No; it's just been one lie after another, and I'm partly to blame ... spoiling him because I couldn't give him a child. I'm thinking of moving back to Rhode Island; it's where I grew up."

"Don't cut yourself off from your friends, Loretta; take a break but don't run away. We're all here to support you."

Hannah didn't know where the well of sympathy had sprung from but Loretta cast such a pathetic figure that even she found it hard not to feel some of the pain, and that was not out of guilt for having been the instigator.

"It worries me that I can't remember going to the office that day. The doctor says I've blanked it out; probably due to the rage of finding out about the contract ... and God knows how I found out about that. I suppose I should be grateful I did; paying the penalties has prevented a very messy legal battle. I would have paid the costs if he'd told me sooner; like I always have ..."

"Then it sounds like it was time for things to move on, Loretta; a fresh start for you both. There is still so much you could do ..."

"A little old to embark on a concert tour, don't you think?"

"Nonsense, and it sounds like just the tonic. Take Dominic with you; it'll be the making of him *and* it'll kick start your own renaissance."

"You say some very wise things for a young woman, Valerie ..."

Was all Loretta said, and Hannah left to pay Jonas one last visit before the casing was due to be delivered.

"It's perfect, Jonas; when can I collect it?"

"The end of the week, Frau Bohm."

"Excellent! And the *Nightingale* looks positively ethereal."

"Over three hundred years old and it looks like it did the day it left *Zenti's* workshop."

"Mrs. Colton will be delighted I'm sure ... especially in light of her current troubles ... How much do I owe you, Jonas?"

"Another five thousand dollars, Frau Bohm."

"I'll have a draft for you on Friday when I collect it."

Chapter Twelve – Could it have turned out any better?

On the Friday of that week, two months after delivering the wreck to Jonas, Hannah collected her harpsichord. She declined the offer for the workshop to deliver it because she didn't want them to know where she lived. She used the travel trolley and by removing the slender legs and stowing it all in the trolley, it was just possible for her to move it by herself. The trolley was *end up* so it looked like a travel case for a harp. Thankfully she only had a harpsichord casing to transport, and that was so much lighter but even she couldn't actually lift it.

She finally managed to get it home with the help of the cab driver and she installed the synthesizer and then tested it to see what effect the old wood had on the sound. In her view, it was an eighty/twenty result but good enough to fool most people who wouldn't have actually heard a harpsichord played live before. The electronic cable exited from the base of the casing and was hidden for the most part by one of the legs.

"Excellent!"

When Dominic came over, he was enthralled, and he played the gala piece of music on it and they both agreed it was as good as they were going to get. She gave him the rudiments of the computer he wanted to build; a box of components that she judged was a fair exchange for his future part in her subterfuge.

A month remained before the *Nightingale* would be ready and there was precious little to do except study of course and teach the occasional music lesson. As a test of her handicraft, she swapped the key she had made for Dominic's own; nothing happened so she assumed it worked, and now she had the means to gain entry to the house.

She re-visited the antique shop in the guise of Anna Bohm and confirmed the delivery date for the harpsichord. The owner was delighted to inform her that he had a buyer lined up, for one hundred and fifty thousand dollars, fully restored.

"There is a warehouse near the airport where the piece should be delivered," he confirmed.

"The piece will be delivered to this shop at noon on that day in exchange for an untraceable bearer bond for one hundred and fifty thousand dollars ..."

"I don't want it seen here."

"I am not taking it to a deserted warehouse."

"If someone sees it come into the shop then when the theft is reported, the police will come straight here."

"Who said it was stolen?"

"It isn't?"

"No ..."

"But it is an Eighteenth-Century Zenti harpsichord, fully restored by Fitzwilliam's?"

"Oh yes ..."

"The *Nightingale* belongs to Loretta Colton."

"Does it?"

"You'll be playing a dangerous game if you double-cross me."

"The threat is noted; but your concern is baseless. You will have what you want and so will I."

Hannah left and smiled richly to herself; if only she could find a decent chess player, she'd give them a run for their money, she mused.

She visited Francine and Charles to confirm the arrangements for the trip to the launch and the flight that Dominic needed to get.

"You're sure you'll manage, Valerie?" asked Francine, the picture of concerned motherhood.

"Absolutely positive; my flight is also booked ..."

"Dominic will be very upset that you're going; he actually looks forward to his lessons with you."

"Once things settle down, he'll be fine, especially if Loretta takes him on tour, and in any event, with your blessing to build the computer, he'll be much happier."

"You'll make a very capable mother one day."

Hannah smiled, leaving the thought hanging.

She visited Loretta. David was absent and she didn't ask where he was; the mood seemed lighter.

"Are you sure the trip to Mexico wouldn't do you the power of good, Loretta?"

"No; it was David's idea. I'm off to the Mojave Desert to find my 'vision'. When I get back, I'll seriously look at the idea of the tour with Dominic, and I may get into these computers myself - shipping is so dull!"

"Is the *Nightingale* ready yet?"

"They say Friday; delivered to the concert venue at three o'clock in the afternoon. I'll see it in the morning when I go and pay their bill!"

"Ouch!"

"Fifty thousand ... but worth every cent and its future is assured."

"I can't wait to play it ... Are you sure you won't play at the gala?"

"Positive; you and Dominic deserve it."

"Thank you ... by the way, who is tuning it once it's delivered to the venue?"

"Oh; do you know, I've completely forgotten about that."

"I'll do it for you."

"You can? I mean; you would?"

"Of course; it would be an honor and in some small way it would repay your debt of kindness."

"Oh dear child; if I had been blessed with a child, I hope it would have been like you."

Hannah left and wondered if Hell would be altogether very terrible or if there was still time to redeem herself!

Now that she knew *the where* and *the when* it was action stations.

On the Friday morning, Loretta went to Fitzwilliam's and paid over fifty thousand dollars, cooed for thirty seconds, and left to get her hair done. Hannah was watching and saw the instrument picked up an hour later by a specialist removal firm that took the harpsichord to the concert venue.

She went home and picked up her harpsichord/synthesizer and took it to the concert venue and, being a concert venue, the sight of a large musical instrument in a travel case did not cause anyone to bat an eye.

Hannah as Valerie set to and tuned the *Nightingale* where it sat on the stage. As it approached lunch, the stagehands made their way to grab a bite and Hannah effected the swap - not without a great deal of effort and a thimble full of sweat but she did it and had hers in position. And just as she hoped, the electrical cable was pretty much hidden and there was an adjacent floor-mounted socket. She played the piece to ensure nothing had gotten damaged in the transfer. All was well, and the sound, compared to the original, which she had just tuned and played, was probably ninety percent there or thereabouts.

She moved the *Nightingale* in the trolley to a dark corner of the backstage area and threw a tarpaulin over it, and then she left.

In the afternoon, she packed and had her two smart cases ready by the door. In the late afternoon and early evening, she got ready for the gala and then went, as arranged, to Dominic's house, so that they could all travel together. Charles had even bought her a corsage. Once at the venue, she and Dominic practiced the all-important piece.

"Why are we playing yours and not Mrs. Colton's?" he asked.

"I think she sold it," said Hannah, "Don't mention anything; she isn't very well."

Dominic, believing he was on the inside track for a change, just winked.

There was a gathering of the great and the good beforehand, ostensibly so that everyone who believed they were somebody could be seen to make their donation, and then everyone took their seats and the evening commenced.

Hannah and Dominic made their entrance onto the stage, and they bowed before taking their positions for the eagerly anticipated duet. Francine and Charles beamed and clapped enthusiastically whilst Loretta just lapped it up; David was nowhere to be seen. They performed the duet, and one supposes because of the occasion and maybe due to the long hours of practising, the piece was received very well. Being as it was Hannah's first original composition, she really dove into it, and Dominic responded and didn't falter once. They received a standing ovation and Hannah played a further piece, solo, as an encore; one of Loretta's favorites.

In the interval, both musicians were in demand and eventually Loretta made it to Hannah's side.

"My dear, that was splendid; young Dominic really has come on under your tutelage. I'm almost positive we will tour once I get back from my vision quest."

"When are you leaving, Loretta?"

"Tomorrow; we're gathering at sunset."

"I shan't see you again," Hannah said with a few tears.

"Oh, don't worry; we'll meet again ... Have fun and don't stop playing!"

"Take care, Loretta; I'm sure everything will work out."

"I know it will."

The evening drew to a close, and Francine and Charles invited Hannah back to the house.

"That's very kind but I have a date, finally!"

"Is he here?" asked Francine, buzzing with anticipation.

"No; he was working this evening; we're meeting for a late supper."

"But if you're leaving, Valerie, what will come of it?"

"He wants to travel, and we'll meet in Europe."

"How romantic!"

Everyone left, and not long afterwards, Hannah was able to effect the switch back, leaving the true *Nightingale* on the stage to be picked up in the morning by the removal firm; to whom Hannah, as Loretta, had spoken, changing the delivery address from the house to the shop with specific orders that it should be delivered at noon. As far as Loretta was concerned, it was being delivered to the house and her housekeeper would be there to receive it. Hannah took the synthesizer home.

The following morning, she dressed as Loretta and went to the shop to make the rendezvous with the delivery of the harpsichord. The owner was a little bewildered to say the least.

"You're selling it, Mrs. Colton?"

"It reminds me too much of David."

"I have a buyer willing to pay one hundred and fifty thousand dollars."

"I'll take it if I can have payment today."

"As it happens, you can."

"Excellent!"

Hannah, as Loretta, took the bond and left the *Nightingale* in the shop but she needed someone other than the shop owner to see her there so that there was at least one independent witness to the sale; Francine came in at the appointed time.

"Loretta!"

"Darling! Can't stop; my "vision" awaits, and it doesn't feature the *Nightingale*, so I've sold it."

"Loretta, surely not!"

"The money will fund the tour - must run, darling. Why are you here?"

"The owner called to say that they had a thimble I might be interested in."

"Goodbye, darling, see you in a month."

Hannah left and grabbed a cab as soon as she could, leaving Francine in a bit of a whirl and when she approached the owner to see the thimble, he didn't have a clue what she was talking about.

Hannah made it to the flat and changed quickly, and then went to Francine's house to stay the evening because they all left the following day.

Francine got back and told Hannah what had happened at the antique shop.

"She looked so fresh, and I swear years have dropped off of her."

"She's becoming a new woman," said Hannah.

Hannah stayed the evening and, in the morning, they went to the airport. She and Dominic, with two of his friends and one of the dads, left for Houston while Charles and Francine went to Mexico. After the launch, she put Dominic on his flight to Mexico as arranged and then flew back to San Francisco. Dressed as Loretta, she went round to Francine's house and let herself in, found the key for the display case in the jewellery box and swapped over the thimbles.

As she left, she made sure that at least one of the neighbours saw her, to whom she waved. Back at the apartment, she waited for the removal firm to pick up her empty, restored harpsichord casing and take it to Loretta's, where the housekeeper took it in and parked it in the small lounge. Hannah then took the synthesizer to one of the better second-hand stores and sold it.

Back at the apartment, she changed back into Hannah and left, taking a cab to the airport from where she flew to New York and thence to London, taking up residence in a small mews house in Chelsea, all under the name of *Virginia Musgrave*.

Epilogue

Nothing, Stateside, happened for about three weeks and the first thing that happened was when Francine went to clean her treasured collection of thimbles for the first time since getting back from Mexico. The shock took a week to get over, and of course, she informed the police, who did their routine enquiries, during which, they happened to speak to the neighbour who had seen Hannah, dressed as Loretta, leave the property that day.

"I'll speak to her," she said to the detective, "She's not been well."

Francine didn't know how to broach the subject, so didn't and for a considerable time thereafter, the subject of thimbles was taboo!

When Loretta got back, she couldn't wait to get the harpsichord out of the travel trolley; momentarily troubled because she didn't remember having a case for it but decided it was a good idea anyway. When the travel trolley was opened, she stood admiring her beloved *Nightingale*. The butler-type took the harpsichord out of the case and sat it down for her. She lifted the lid and once the fact that the case was minus its innards registered, she actually fainted. The police did visit the antique shop and were told, with some measure of satisfaction by the owner, that Loretta herself had sold it to him; a fact that could be verified by Mrs. Francine Eagleton. A fact which was verified, and after that, Loretta went straight back to the Mojave Desert.

Fitzwilliam's confirmed that the case which stood in Loretta's parlour had been restored by them, for Frau Anna Bohm; and there the trail led nowhere for there was no record of her anywhere and no one by that name had left on a flight in the period since.

Dominic added two and two together, being a bright lad, but seeing as he'd witnessed the launch of the *Columbia* and got to build his beloved computer, he reckoned that they were a fair trade for keeping his mouth tight shut; nor did he have to tour with Loretta and that guaranteed his silence.

Crime Six - Rivals

Chapter One – The Quarrel

Hannah sat and meditated; she blamed it on the slight guilt trip she was having for pushing Loretta a little too far over the edge with the masquerade in San Francisco. Then again, Loretta could always blame David and his antics if a scapegoat was required. Posing as Loretta to sell the harpsichord and avoid the dangerous handover had worked beautifully, and in fact, no 'crime' had been committed; the one hundred and fifty thousand dollars made a handsome addition to her pension fund. The identities of *Valerie Bishop* and *Anna Bohm* had also remained intact. She had the thimble and stealing that from Francine was a bonus; it had been opportunistic and wholly personal. She had no intention of selling the thimble; quite the opposite, she was sure that the thimble must be part of a *'necessaire de couture'*, and fully intended to find the other pieces along with the case. But that was an aside to the main act which she now contemplated.

As soon as she'd arrived in London, she had contacted Boehme, and he'd been absolutely delighted to hear from her; less so when she had asked him for a referral. The secrets that she still held onto, which kept him in her vice-like grip, persuaded him to let her have a name.

"*Forbes Darlington*; he is a collector; nothing stands in his way when he decides that he wants something ... and he *wants* the 'Medici Quartet'..."

"Does he? Well; I shall get it for him."

"Please be careful; he isn't dangerous like Manuel but dangerous nevertheless, and he has a very long reach."

"Have no fear, and after this, perhaps we should meet and I'll give you back the evidence I stole from your receptionist's desk that day."

"The pleasure of seeing you would be enough, *mademoiselle*."

"Until then ..."

"A serious collector after the fabled 'Medici Quartet' *but* how much does he want it?" Hannah mused.

The 'Medici Quartet' was a painting of, needless to say, four musicians. It had been painted for Elizabeth the First, who had gifted it to a noble family whose remnants still resided in Kent, in the Tudor manor house on the outskirts of Chilham - blood so blue, you could dip your quill in it.

The painting was priceless due to its provenance and age, and during the summer, the family opened its doors and welcomed the hordes in, demanding a princely sum to see the painting and various other heirlooms.

"A smash and grab over the cucumber sandwiches and Earl Grey? No; something more subtle ..."

Step one was to contact the collector - Forbes Darlington - to see just how much he wanted it. Hannah donned the cloak of disguise; in this case, *Virginia Musgrave*, an art historian and a gallery owner. She'd rented a tidy little shop on the Kings Road and planned to open a gallery. Why go to the bother of breaking into people's houses and stealing their art when they were willing to bring it to you?

Spending one hundred thousand pounds very judiciously on Elizabethan art, having tracked Forbes' recent purchases, Hannah had detected a shift in his collecting habits towards music related subjects. She'd outbid him on one particular lot, and it formed the centerpiece of the exhibition that she put on for the opening of the gallery. On the day of the opening, a well-dressed man came in, and she knew he must be Forbes' agent.

"The 'Quarrel'..." was all he said.

"An excellent example of his work; recently sold at auction for twice the reserve. I believe Forbes Darlington was interested ..."

"I believe so ... I have a client who is very interested in acquiring it."

"It is not for sale-"

"Oh!"

"The owner very graciously donated it for the purposes of the exhibition ..."

"Are you sure they could not be persuaded to reconsider?"

"Of course, that's possible, but it is merely a week since the sale, so hardly likely - I could ask. After the exhibition, it is traveling to Kent to be included in the annual *Fotherington Show*; the subject being sympathetic to the 'Quartet', and it is believed that 'The Quarrel' was painted as a kind of homage to the great piece. It will be the first time they have been seen together ..."

"Yes; the connection is well documented. Sadly, my client is unable to attend the show this year."

"That is a pity."

"If you would ask the owner to reconsider, my client is extremely keen to acquire the piece."

"I will ask, but I doubt anything will change until after the show and it is possible that the painting will remain there as part of the permanent display."

"Please ask."

"I will. Is there anything else your client is interested in? 'The Maplin' for example?"

"He has 'The King's Men', so not likely."

This was the slip that Hannah had been waiting for.

"So, your client is *Forbes Darlington* ..."

The man coloured and fumbled for an escape route, which Hannah provided.

"I own 'The Quarrel', and if Forbes is that interested then he need only call in himself and I would be prepared to discuss terms."

"He doesn't usually deal directly."

"I always do ... and if he is going to miss the show at *Fotherington* then perhaps that will provide the added incentive."

"I'll be in touch Ms.?"

"Virginia Musgrave ..."

He left and Hannah felt very pleased with her performance.

Chapter Two – Forbes Darlington

Hannah estimated that it would be about a week before Forbes would be in touch. She opened the gallery each day and waited patiently. Ten days after the first visit, his agent re-appeared at three o'clock in the afternoon.

"Ms. Musgrave."

"Alistair."

"Forbes will deal direct, but he insists that you visit him at his home."

"When?"

"This Saturday, he has invited you to dine, should you be free."

"I would be delighted to accept the invitation, and I shall bring 'The Quarrel' with me; what time?"

"Seven o'clock; his driver can collect you."

"Call it independence or just capriciousness, but I will make my own way there. Please pass on my thanks to Forbes."

"Good day, Ms. Musgrave."

"Goodbye, Alistair."

"Bingo!" Hannah allowed herself a rare moment of self-congratulation. "Forbes is not only an avaricious collector but a recluse, tucked up in his pile in Tadworth, sending forth minions like Alistair to get their hands grubby on his behalf. A personal invitation to dine with him; he is obviously serious and maybe more than a little curious about me ..."

At the appointed time, Hannah arrived at the gates of the house in Tadworth - 'Rosebriars' - and within thirty seconds, the gates opened automatically. She drove up to the house over the pristine gravel. She had rented a Jaguar XK150 drop head coupe. A business had opened in Chelsea renting out exotic sports cars; the car looked the part and it had been relatively inexpensive. Alistair came out to greet her.

"Ms. Musgrave ..."

"Please call me *Virginia* ..."

"Virginia ... Forbes is so pleased you could make it. Did you bring the painting?"

"Of course ..."

Hannah retrieved the painting from the boot of the car, and they went into what Hannah could only describe as *The Victoria and Albert Museum*, but all of the artwork was Elizabethan and some of it was much earlier.

"I never knew Forbes had such a thing for the *Golden Era*," Hannah said as they passed through the hall into the main salon.

"He sees it as his duty to preserve the art of the period for future generations ..."

"Does he still have the *Hapsworth* miniature?"

"I most certainly do!" came the shrill reply from behind them, and both turned to see Forbes standing at the foot of the stairs; a 'Kenneth Williams' character dressed for dinner, sporting a dickie bow. "Ms. Musgrave; the pleasure is all mine ..." he added and stepped forward except that he did not hold out his hand for hers.

"Please call me Virginia. As promised, I brought 'The Quarrel'-"

"Later; sherry?"

"Thank you ..."

Alistair hovered while a butler served the drinks.

"Alistair; be a good chap and fetch the miniature for Virginia to see." Turning to Hannah, he said, "I haven't shown the *Hapsworth* miniature to anyone for more than twenty years."

"I'm honoured that you should choose me."

"You brought the painting ... I do hope we can agree on terms."

"Of that I have no doubt," said Hannah just as Alistair brought in the miniature for her to see. It was kept in a Morocco leather case which Alistair set down on the table. Forbes retrieved a key from his pocket and unlocked it, lifting the lid to reveal the miniature of Elizabeth the First that had been painted in her coronation year and in which she was dressed in the royal regalia.

"No one knows who painted it. It turned up when Henry sold *Hapsworth* to pay his father's death duties; I stepped in to avoid seeing it go East ... that was thirty years ago now."

Hannah was leaning over the box and peering at the portrait of the young queen. Even in a painting of that size, the eyes appeared to gaze back at her.

"Mesmerizing," she breathed, "Thank you; this is a rare treat and one I won't forget for a very long time."

Shortly after that, the box was locked up and Alistair took it away.

"It'll probably be another twenty years before it sees the light of day again ... Shall we eat?"

"Yes," smiled Hannah, feeling uncommonly relaxed.

They entered the dining room. The table was set just for two; Alistair didn't return.

"Why did you outbid me for 'The Quarrel'?"

"To see how much you wanted it."

"I want it very much."

"It's going to the *Fotherington Show* next week."

"Name your price and leave it here tonight."

"I have a better offer for you."

"Young lady; there can be no better offer."

"The 'Medici Quartet'..."

"What of it?"

"You want that too."

"Yes; but I'm never likely to get it ..."

"How much would you be prepared to pay for the pleasure of having it?"

"With good title? Half a million; without, two hundred thousand pounds."

"You'd willingly pay two hundred thousand pounds for a painting you couldn't admit to owning, and if it was stolen from the

Fotherington Show, everyone knows you want it so all fingers would point here ... that's a hell of a risk you'd be prepared to take ..."

"Virginia; I have wanted that piece for as long as I can remember. The empty space where it would hang is like a demon taunting me ... it completes the collection, along with 'The Quarrel'..."

"And the 'Maplin'?"

"An inferior piece compared to 'The King's Men'..."

"Still; all together they would be magnificent."

"You have two of them; are you suggesting to me that I can have them all?"

"For half a million pounds you can have them all *and* 'The Medici Quartet' would come with good title ..."

"I don't believe you can persuade James to sell it; without it, there is no *Fotherington*!"

"Let *me* worry about that ... Are we agreed; half a million pounds for all three paintings?"

"... 'The Quarrel', 'The Maplin' and 'The Medici Quartet', along with my 'The King's Men' would complete a life's work; there would be no finer collection."

"So?"

"You have my word; half a million pounds with good title. Can you leave 'The Quarrel' tonight?"

"Only if you show me the 'Ann Boleyn With Child'..."

"Ms. Musgrave; that painting has never been seen by anyone else alive today."

"I know ... but I want to see it."

Forbes possessed a painting of Ann Boleyn painted during her confinement with Elizabeth; it was a rare and candid portrait of a young woman who believed she would have it all. The parallel was a little too obvious for Hannah but fine art was becoming like a drug to her; almost as potent and addictive as stealing it!

"Follow me," said Forbes, and he got up and waited for Hannah to reach his side of the table before escorting her to an interior room on an upper floor, which was windowless and panelled in rich oak. The heavy door was locked of course, and the key was itself locked away in a chamber which Forbes darted into en route. The painting was behind a solid box frame, which itself was locked, and Forbes carried *that* key with him at all times. He seemed to *re-join* her as he unlocked it, having retreated somewhat since making the offer.

"This painting started my collection. It nearly bankrupted me then; all my hopes were hung with it. I have to say, I fared better than she; much like the infant she was carrying ... of course her future was uncertain as was mine until history took its fateful turn ..."

"How different history could have been," injected Hannah.

"Quite!"

"Thank you ..."

"No one else will see this until after I die; if you do not get me 'The Medici Quartet' I will have you killed ..."

"If you threaten me, Forbes, I will steal this and burn it on the lawn in front of the house."

"I believe you would ... I have no fear that you won't get me what I want."

They returned to the salon for coffee, and Alistair made a re-appearance.

"Alistair; 'The Quarrel' remains with us ... Be so kind as to show Virginia out; I will retire now ..."

He left and Alistair looked expectantly at Hannah.

"Collect 'The Maplin' at your leisure, Alistair." Hannah said, "I will deliver 'The Medici Quartet' after the *Fotherington Show*, in four weeks. Upon delivery, I require an untraceable bearer bond for five hundred thousand pounds ..."

"Splendid, Ms. Musgrave; I believe you know what Forbes will do if you fail him."

"And he knows what *I* shall do if he fails me ... Goodnight."

"Goodnight."

Hannah drove back to the mews cottage in Chelsea while her stomach alternately flipped back and forth; the stakes could not be higher or the adrenalin course through her veins any quicker!

Chapter Three – James Fotherington

Hannah had contacted James Fotherington just before the opening of the gallery to see, very tongue in cheek, if he would loan the 'Quartet' for the purposes of the exhibition. But not even Hannah's ample charms and the other two paintings that she planned to exhibit alongside it could persuade James to relinquish the 'Quartet' even for a day; the painting had never left the house in Chilham since the day that Elizabeth had gifted it to the family.

Being good natured, he did suggest that perhaps she could loan 'The Quarrel' for the show, and that was how it was left. Clearly that was not possible now but the game had many levels; just as Forbes was hell-bent on acquiring 'The Medici Quartet', James was equally keen to acquire the 'Ann Boleyn With Child'. He considered *Fotherington* to be its rightful home.

Rivals make for such interesting sport!

The day after the dinner with Forbes, Hannah telephoned James to apologize for the fact that the 'Quarrel' would not be coming after all.

"I'm so sorry, James. Forbes made a silly offer conditional on the painting being delivered immediately, along with 'The Maplin'; I couldn't refuse."

"I understand perfectly, Virginia; Forbes can be very persuasive, *and* he has exceedingly deep pockets."

"I traded for a peek at the 'Ann Boleyn With Child'; it seemed only fair."

"And he showed you?!"

"Of course ... I can be equally persuasive, James."

"Of that, I have no doubt ... but that painting has not been seen by another living soul."

"It has now ... He only wants the 'Quartet' to complete his life's work. I believe he will expire if all the paintings were finally together at Rosebriars."

"Quite possibly; are you still coming to the show?"

"Oh yes; I wouldn't miss it for the world ... and I can tell you about the *Hapsworth* miniature too-"

"Good God! Did you have him eating out of your palm as well?"

"Not exactly ... See you next week, James; I'm staying locally so perhaps we could have dinner one evening."

"I'm sure we can manage that; goodbye, Virginia."

"Bye, James ..."

Forbes was right; there would be no *Fotherington* without the painting, and the annual show, which lasted a week, drew a modest crowd. The money kept the house but very little else. James was actually quite poorly off though he would never admit to it.

"He really needs the 'Boleyn' to put *Fotherington* on the map and safeguard his future, but he has no money and he didn't even bid for 'The Quarrel'. With the future of the house looking so uncertain these days, I wonder just how desperate he is ..."

Hannah drove down in the Jaguar and checked into the local hotel for a few nights, calling in on James the following morning, one day before the show opened. The house was busy and James looked harassed.

"Not there, there!" he was screaming when Hannah arrived, and she smiled encouragingly as he turned around.

"Virginia?"

"Yes, it is. Hello, James."

He shook her hand warmly and escorted her to his study for a coffee.

"It gets harder every year, I swear it."

"This will be my first time ..."

"It's rather quaint in its way. I can't stand the thought of the house being open all year round; just for a week is bearable - small, select crowds and no coaches!"

"But no tourist dollars or yen either, James ..."

"No ..." he replied wistfully, "Still; it doesn't always have to be about the money, does it?"

"No; you're right, but it can't be any cheaper to maintain this property year-on-year."

"Quite the opposite; it's getting damn expensive, and you can't find the craftsmen these days."

Their conversation went on in a similar vein for half an hour, until James asked, "Do you want to see the 'Quartet' before the hordes?"

"Oh, James; really? That would be wonderful ..."

He towed her to a library-style room. The painting was on an easel, propped up in a corner.

"Not locked away like the 'Boleyn'..." Hannah remarked.

"I can't believe he showed it to you. I've asked - even offered to pay - but he has refused point blank."

"You didn't have 'The Quarrel' to offer in fair trade."

"If I had those paintings, all together, what a show we would have then!"

"What would you give to have all those paintings, James?"

"Your tone suggests that you were asking seriously."

"I was ..."

"Half a million; it's all that's left in the kitty. It'll see me to the grave if I'm lucky, but then everything will go unless I do something."

"For half a million I will get you, with good title, all the paintings that you want, which includes 'The Maplin', 'The King's Men', 'The Quarrel' *and* the 'Boleyn'..."

"You're jesting; he won't part with any of them ... not willingly."

"Maybe not *willingly*, but part with them he will."

"Get me the paintings and I'll pay you half a million."

"Deal! Shall we have dinner tonight? My treat; the hotel's menu is pretty good."

"I would be delighted."

"Eight o'clock."

"See you then."

"Bye ..."

They did dine; both flirted outrageously and their tinkle of laughter was heard all evening.

"Good night, James. I'll see you tomorrow, and if you truly want all the paintings then I will get them for you ..."

"I do; but I don't see how you can, not with good title. He'd burn them on the front lawn before he parted with them ..."

Hannah just smiled as she gave him a tender little kiss on the cheek.

"Patience, James; we all get what we want in the end ... Sleep tight."

James went back to *Fotherington* euphoric if not a little bemused. A nut of certainty was growing in the pit of his stomach that something would - had to - happen, and to finally best Forbes and be able to show all the paintings would be the culmination of his own life's work. Christ: he might even allow coaches!

Hannah went upstairs very happy with her progress. All she needed to do now was to decide which of these vain arses she was going to make triumphal and who was least likely to bear a grudge. That would seem to be James *but* it was all too easy to fall for the faded gentility and quaintness; both had the money, so it boiled down to which one represented the least risk on her part.

"Of course, Hannah, you could always alleviate them both of their burdens and double your takings ..."

Hannah didn't know who this inner voice belonged to. She mused that she must be the reincarnation of some great art thief; whoever it was seemed to be looking out for her interests, so she didn't mind.

Chapter Four – The Fotherington Show

Hannah had breakfast, freshened up, and then walked the relatively short distance to the house for the show which opened its doors at eleven o'clock. Having seen the painting the day before, she didn't really need to go, but having promised James, she put her best foot forward.

The car park was full by the time she got to the house, and being the first day of the annual show, it was bustling. The tour was lead through the lower portion of the house, and in one room - the big study - the painting was now on display, protected behind a thick silk cordon. Security was deliberately understated but if the painting was moved, the alarms went off and the hounds of hell were let loose. Everyone shuffled past in orderly fashion and in near silence. No photographs were permitted but prints in three sizes were available in the small gift shop. James just hovered, pressing palms with regular *goers* and smiling all the time - also mentally totting up the takings and whether the leaky roof would finally be fixed this year.

Hannah paid and toured; it meant she saw the rest of the collection, which was impressive if a little thin in parts.

"Virginia! Good morning: a splendid turn out as you can see," said James, catching up with her as she got to the end.

"Well done, James, and the best of luck with the rest of the week; I'll be in touch in about two weeks."

"Okay ... I'm feeling quite sick with the anticipation; promise me this isn't a cruel joke."

"This isn't a cruel joke ... By the way, what service did the family render the Queen that brought about the gift in the first place?"

A shadow passed across James's face; it was almost undetectable but, in that nanosecond, Hannah knew that what he was about to say was going to be a complete lie.

"Immediately after the defeat of the Armada the nation needed ships, and my ancestor, Henry Fotherington, provided a large quantity of the timber that was required to rebuild the fleet ..."

"Fascinating period of our history I always think," ventured Hannah.

"Yes, it is ..."

She left shortly afterward, having the feeling that he knew that she knew that he had told a lie. Since the family name, the estate and its fortunes were built on this story, it was going to take more than a little delving to ferret out the truth.

"No one said that this job was easy, Hannah," she mused.

Before she left the village, Hannah visited the family graveyard and took a large number of photographs. It wasn't immediately apparent where the flaw lay but it was there somewhere. After a brief visit to Rochester, she returned to London and headed for the gallery, which had been closed. Two letters were in the post box; the first a bill for the electricity and the second from Forbes Darlington, which read -

'Dear Virginia,

I hope you are enjoying the show. Did you inform James it would be his last? I suspect not. Alistair will call on Thursday to pick up 'The Maplin' and I expect the 'Quartet' to be delivered a week after that, <u>Friday at the latest</u>. Come to dinner; I am relishing listening to the story of how you prised the painting out of James' clutches and got good title to it.

Adieu!

Forbes.'

"Smug bastard ..."

It was late by now and the journey had been tiring so she went straight to bed and began to recall the names of the Fotherington's since the first - Henry - in preference to counting sheep.

Chapter Five – Where historians fear to tread

Research was bread and butter to Hannah, and she was extremely thorough. With her orderly mind and her knack for seeing connections, it took two days and a morning at the Records' Office to find the key to why James Fotherington was attempting to 'touch up' his portrait.

"Ah!" was all Hannah allowed herself at the time of the final discovery.

Thursday came and 'The Maplin' was picked up by Alistair.

"A week tomorrow, Virginia."

"I hope that isn't Forbes' way of frightening me."

"Just a gentle reminder."

"None is needed, and if he does it again, I'll burn the *Boleyn* in front of his eyes ... I'll see you next week on Friday - oh! Could you tell Forbes that the *Hapsworth* miniature is most likely a fake? Henry's father did own the miniature but sold it surreptitiously before the end. A colleague of mine has stumbled across something. By next Friday, I'll know for sure if he did sell it *and* to whom ... If I'm able to confirm that, then Forbes can no doubt sue Henry and get his money back."

"Friday will prove to be an interesting day all round."

"Goodbye, Alistair ..."

Hannah had relayed the information to rattle Forbes; she had no idea if the miniature was fake or genuine ... yet!

She donned her new disguise to see how it suited her; an older woman, perhaps forty, regal, noble - a lady, a *Fotherington,* and one demanding her rightful inheritance. Hannah had the proof that James was not all *Fotherington* - quite the bastard in fact, and *Lady Jane Fotherington* was about to bring an end to his little charade.

The real *Lady Jane Fotherington* was in an asylum in Switzerland; a fact that was not widely known. Hannah rented a Mercedes sports car and drove down to *Fotherington* on the last day of the show. Choosing her moment carefully, to make the biggest scene possible, she announced her arrival and demanded to know why the house was full of strangers and where the devil was James. He was hurriedly found.

"Lady Jane?"

"Yes, James! The very same; cured and back for what is rightfully mine!"

"But *Fotherington* is my home. What about the show; the painting?"

"Keep the house but I want the painting!" she hurled back.

"The painting has never left this house; it is the centrepiece of the collection. The show is the highlight of the calendar; you can't take it-"

"I can and I will! No little bastard is going to stop me. If that painting is not put into the boot of my car within the hour, I will publicize your grubby little *heritage*, and after that there will be nothing!"

"Please, Jane; you'll ruin me. The house costs a fortune to maintain, and the coffers are empty."

"If you give me the painting then I'll give you the *Hapsworth* miniature."

"But you don't have it; Henry sold it to Forbes Darlington to pay his father's death duties."

"It wasn't his to sell."

"You honestly think Forbes will hand it over to you?"

"He has no choice, and if he doesn't, then I'll publicize his part in the ruse."

"Take the painting *but* I must have the miniature."

"You will - by the end of next week. Update, James; change the formula *and* I would seriously think about selling up."

James had the painting packed and put into the boot of the Mercedes.

"I'll see you next week, James; don't look so downhearted, you'll have the miniature ..."

Hannah drove off and headed back to the gallery to 'sell' the painting to Virginia Musgrave for half a million pounds, after which, *Lady Jane* went back to Switzerland to re-commence her treatment. Hannah as *Virginia* had good title to the painting and the payment for the painting was simply made by transferring the amount out of one of her accounts into another that she had.

She called Alistair.

"Alistair; I have the painting. Do you have the bond ready?"

"Certainly, Virginia; Forbes is going to be delighted if not astounded. Did you receive confirmation that the miniature was a fake?"

"Yes, I did. The original sale took place before Henry's father died; he sold it to Jane Fotherington-"

"Did he?!"

"I have a letter from her confirming that she still has it."

"Forbes is very unhappy about this as you can imagine."

"I'm sure ... Still, he has 'The Medici Quartet' now, and I'm sure that will make it all right."

"When are you bringing it over?"

"Tomorrow at around eleven o'clock."

"Perfect!"

"Oh, Alistair; if Forbes thinks he is going to play any games then remind him, gently, what I will do."

"There will be no games I can assure you."

"Good; see you tomorrow."

Chapter Six – Incendiary Device

The following day at eleven o'clock, Hannah, as Virginia, in the rented Jaguar, went over to Forbes', and as soon as the gate was opened, she sped up the driveway before either Alistair or Forbes had made it out of the house to greet her. She had the painting set upon an easel beside the car, next to which was a petrol can.

Forbes himself came out.

"Virginia; why the theatricals?"

"Oh; call it feminine intuition, Forbes. I want the bond and the miniature else I'm going to set this alight-"

"Please do not do anything rash or stupid; Alistair is fetching the miniature and your payment."

"Good!"

Alistair came out with the case which housed the miniature and an envelope that contained the bond for half a million pounds.

"Place them on the ground right there," said Hannah, pointing to patch on the driveway, "then retreat ..."

"There really is no need for this, Virginia; we're delighted that you have delivered the painting."

"It matters not - back off!"

They did, and she checked the bond and then opened the case to find the miniature inside.

"Excellent! Here is your copy of the letter from Jane Fotherington, confirming that she still has the miniature."

"How did you get James to relinquish 'The Quartet'?" asked Forbes.

"Oh; that was easy once I had established that he didn't have title to it in the first place; he couldn't hand it over quickly enough to avoid any embarrassment."

"So, who did?"

"Jane."

"Why did she part with it?"

"She wanted you to have the collection, Forbes; she's hoping that you decide to show the paintings - maybe even just a one-off show?"

"Well, perhaps I will, by way of a celebration ... and what of James?"

"I expect he'll sell *Fotherington* now and quietly disappear."

"This has worked out far better than I hoped; notwithstanding the miniature, but then I'll get my money back eventually and I'll buy the *Greshing*."

"Goodbye, Forbes ... Alistair ..."

Hannah got back into the car and drove down the driveway towards the gates, which did not open immediately; she waited. Eventually, they did open, and she waved as she drove out; it had been touch and go all along. Her relief in not having to ram the gates and pay out for the damages to the car was palpable.

She drove to the airport and handed over the keys to the car to the chap from the garage. After loading her two smart cases onto a trolley, she headed into departures for the short flight to Paris and a long-awaited reunion with Boheme. Not only did he welcome her with open arms but in exchange for the return of certain documents, he found a buyer for the miniature *and* a new client.

"The *Veronese*?"

"Something worthy of your talents at last ..."

"All roads lead to Rome ..."